A GATHERING PLACE

A GATHERING PLACE

VICKI SALLOUM

This is a work of fiction. Some characters were inspired by memories of the author's relatives, but all are ultimately products of the imagination. Aunt Cracker, honored in the dedication, is the only figure specifically acknowledged. Any likeness to other real people, places, or events is entirely coincidental.

ISBNs: # 979-8-9990422-8-6 (paperback); # 979-8-9990422-9-3 (ebook)

Library of Congress Control Number: # 2025946361

First Printing: 2025

Printed in the United States of America

PRAISE FOR VICKI SALLOUM

Mississippi native and resident of New Orleans, Vicki Salloum has magically woven her Lebanese Catholic family's colorful roots and traditions into a wonderful piece of literary fiction in her novel, *A Gathering Place*. There's plenty of tension as Blue and her niece Jamila deal with racism, the ongoing threat of violence, and resistance from their family, but that tension is offset by the myriad of beautiful descriptions of the language, music, and food of three races, Lebanese, Latino, and African American. The reader joins with all three groups as they learn from each other and face the future together. Filled with hope and redemption, *A Gathering Place* will capture your heart.

— SUSAN CUSHMAN, AUTHOR OF *JOHN AND MARY MARGARET* AND *TANGLES AND PLAQUES: A MOTHER AND DAUGHTER FACE ALZHEIMER'S*

Vicki Salloum's *A Gathering Place* is a sophisticated multicultural family saga following the life of Blue—an elderly lady full of tenacity and passion as she follows a voice she heard from the Mother of God to rebuild a community. Using the remnants of memories after Hurricane Katrina to construct a future of love and a sense of place where all are welcomed, Blue is on a journey of faith and conviction. Filled with spirituality and holy dreams, Salloum writes to provide hope for all in overcoming obstacles and struggles of every size, giving a soul to these pages. All it takes is just one person. Blue.

— SHOME DASGUPTA, AUTHOR OF *CAJUN SOUTH BROWN FOLK*

An entertaining and poignant addition to the post-Katrina canon of New Orleans stories. *A Gathering Place* takes us inside a loving family, complete with inter-generational drama, joyful and tragic memories, and delicious Lebanese food. The author takes on some complex racial and socio-economic dynamics, wrapping them into a lively and sometimes madcap plot with tenderness, music, and poetry. It's rare we get an octogenarian protagonist with this kind of drive and determination—Blue's story will touch your heart.

— ELISA M. SPERANZA, AUTHOR OF *THE ITALIAN PRISONER*

Vicki Salloum celebrates her heritage and her beloved city of New Orleans in this engaging story of Aunt Blue, a woman driven by faith and a mission: to revive a lost corner of post-Katrina New Orleans. With skillful prose, vivid characters, affectionate humor, and a page-turning pace, *A Gathering Place* shines a light on the cultural gumbo that is New Orleans.

— Carolyn Perry, Author of *For Better, For Worse: Patient in the Maelstrom*

In memory of my mom, dad, and
Aunt Cracker, the inspiration for Aunt Blue

But soon we shall die and all memory of those five will have left the earth, and we ourselves shall be loved for a while and forgotten. But the love will have been enough; all those impulses of love return to the love that made them. Even memory is not necessary for love. There is a land of the living and a land of the dead and the bridge is love, the only survival, the only meaning.

— THE BRIDGE OF SAN LUIS REY, THORNTON WILDER

CHAPTER 1

"*Sabah alkheir*, Jamila."

It was a surprise hearing her voice on the phone, delivered in the exaggeratedly regal, fun-loving style that was uniquely hers. I hadn't talked to her since the funeral and assumed she was still in Jeremiah, following the death of her brother, Fayad.

"Blue, is that you? *Good morning!*" I cried.

All of us nieces, nephews, and step-kids called her that, ever since we were little, despite her delicate (yet desperate) attempts to get us to call her by her birth name, Bahia Bechara. I am fifty-one years old and can still remember the day she came to us, when I was only six, right after Aunt Nayla died and Uncle Imad married her and brought her to Harbortown. That was forty-five years ago. And now Blue was eighty-one.

"What a surprise! Great to hear from you!"

"Guess where I am," she said.

"Where?"

"New Orleans."

"No kidding? How did you get here?"

"By bus. I'm at the terminal."

I can count on one hand the number of times Blue had visited, and only after I'd invited her to my Easter parties, but never following Katrina. In the four years since the storm, her life had been one big two-way bus ride from Harbortown, on the Mississippi Gulf Coast, to Jeremiah, in the Mississippi Delta, unless she was lucky enough to catch a ride with family.

"What are you doing here?"

"It's a long story," she said. "I'll tell you when we can sit down."

"Can you come over, Blue? What are your plans? Who's picking you up?"

"Well, nobody," she laughed nervously. "I was hoping you could."

"Of course, I'll be right over. Meet me outside."

It was May—bright and sunny. And Sunday, so I didn't have to work. All I had on schedule were a few household chores, and I was thrilled at the thought of seeing Blue. I hung up, put on my jeans, and rushed downtown to the bus station.

I couldn't figure out what she was doing here.

This was something Blue never did. She was forever surrounded by loved ones, whether in Harbortown, where she had a million friends and church buddies and family, or in Jeremiah, where she'd grown up with her siblings and cousins, all living in one big house. Nobody in the Kaddoura family ever married, except for Aunt Nayla and Blue, both to the same man, and so they'd remained in that house as adults, close and loving and proud.

There was a school across the street where they were educated, and their family-owned department store was only a few blocks away. The Catholic church where they attended Mass was also across the street. Blue's gigantic Lebanese

Catholic family, with its gentility, small-town closeness and cherished community ties, reminded me of the characters in Faulkner's *A Rose for Emily*, except no one in that family ever slept with a dead corpse, at least not that I could tell.

The point is, Blue was never alone.

When I think of her, I think about her New Year's Eve parties, attended by hundreds of kinfolk from as far away as North Carolina. Or her rosary prayer sessions that had been going on for decades. Until the storm, I don't think she missed one. Or the weekends spent with us kids—my brothers and all my cousins—jammed together around her "breakfast" table, eating *kibbi nayye* and stuffed grape leaves steamed in her silver pressure cooker and picked from the vines she grew in her side yard.

Now, here she was outside the New Orleans bus terminal, three suitcases by her side. I stopped the car, put them in the trunk, and brought Blue to my house. I helped her up the front steps. She sat in an armchair and rested her feet on the ottoman. She looked tired, so I offered iced tea. I sat on my crushed blue velvet sofa, propped my feet on the coffee table, and asked, "What are you doing here?"

"It's something I decided after Fayad died." She gazed across the room, lost in her myriad thoughts. "I'm here to start a new life."

She sipped her tea.

"It's been four years since the storm," she added, "and one by one they've all gone." She seemed to be talking about her family in Jeremiah.

"I'm so sorry about your brother, Blue."

I'd attended her brother's funeral the previous month. I'd driven to Harbortown to meet my brothers and sisters-in-law, and together we traveled the six-hour trek to Jeremiah, stopping only once for sandwiches. We passed cotton fields, sugarcane fields and cow pastures before reaching the

Mississippi Delta town. I'd done my practice teaching in Jeremiah when I was in college, but the town had drastically changed since then. All we found was a strip of boarded-up storefronts—a nearly desolate downtown—and poor folks milling about gas stations. It broke my heart to see how death had crept in. The priest said a few words at the cemetery, and we went to the church hall to eat a church-prepared meal. In the old days, when Blue's kin were still alive, one could count on a sumptuous home-cooked Middle Eastern feast served on an elaborate banquet table, with mourners coming from miles around to spend the day with the Kaddoura family in their enormous ancestral home. Now, everybody was gone.

"It was a lovely funeral," I said.

"I put our home up for sale, Jamila. Not that anyone's going to buy it. And I'm planning on living here."

"Here? You mean New Orleans?"

"I'm going to buy a property. To start a business, honey."

"A property?"

Blue focused on her tea. "It'll be a place where Lebanese families can come. There'll be Lebanese food and music for dancing, if that's what they want to do. And we'll visit with each other. It'll be a home away from home." Hollows appeared under her eyes; she seemed way down, deep in the dumps. "It'll be the center of activity for the Lebanese community. No one's done that before, as far as I can see."

I sensed hope struggling to resurrect itself, but it lay back down and went to sleep.

"How long have you been planning this, Blue?"

"I've done a lot of thinking, sitting in Fayad's hospital room." Absently, she rattled the ice in her tea. "At first, all I could think about was the deaths—Shada, Josephine, Reem—all coming one after the other. Of course, Ellis and Adnan went long before that. But it seemed that after the storm, everything... stepped up. *Ya haram,* poor Shada gets sick... then Josephine and Reem break down..."

She pressed her cheek against the back of the chair. "I thought how much I missed them," she murmured. "I thought about the good times we had, the beautiful parties over all the years." She sat up and continued, "The parties began to occupy a special place in my heart. I began obsessing about them. Then planning them. Every detail, in my head. Who I'd invite—who was left after all these years? —what food I'd serve, what music for dancing, when I'd need to send out the invitations, and what would be the next occasion. I had no real plan to do any of it. Just thinking about it made me happy. It was a way of keeping sane and my mind off Fayad's suffering."

Blue leaned back, her face strained. "And then... he died, that's when something... unusual... happened."

"What?"

Blue's eyes grew shiny, and a faint glow came over her. She gave a short, nervous laugh. "Darlin', you must think I'm crazy, don't you?"

"No, of course not."

"And so," she went on haltingly, face seamed with fatigue, "the orders... came in. At first, I rejected them. But..."—she smiled mysteriously—"I was convincingly persuaded. And so I was to come here to New Orleans to start my business."

"What are you talking about? What orders?"

"Why, orders from the Mother of God."

~

I can remember the day Blue first came to Harbortown, the day I first laid eyes on her. I couldn't have been more than six years old when Uncle Imad brought her from Jeremiah. And she must have been thirty-seven. She was beautiful, with blue eyes. And she came to my house and introduced herself as Bahia Bechara. She stayed a while in our kitchen to chat, making my brothers and me feel special. When she told us her name, I sensed how much it meant to her to be called that: Aunt Bahia. But in the days after her arrival, someone—most likely a child who couldn't pronounce her name—must have called her Blueberry. Soon it was shortened, the adults picked it up, and she was stuck with that name forever.

She and Uncle Imad and his three kids, Rima, Sally Ann, and Elie—once her nieces and nephew, now her step-kids—lived in the red-brick house next door to me. My house was a three-story white Colonial on the beachfront of the Mississippi Coast. More times than I can remember, my brothers and I would run over in our pajamas to Aunt Blue's house next door to eat hot fried dough buried under an avalanche of powdered sugar. Once, I sat in her kitchen devouring ice cream she'd made from snow on the jaw-dropping day it snowed in Harbortown.

In the years following the death of Blue's sister and Blue's marriage to Uncle Imad, she became a second mother to us all: Rima, Sally Ann, and Elie; me and my two brothers; and my Aunt Marcia's twins, Meredith and Michael. Blue also became my mom's best friend. That was before Katrina slammed into our coastal towns and messed up her life forever.

"Blue," I said after a silence, "you received orders from *who?*"

"The Mother of God. I'm to prepare a gathering place. And I will be living in it as well."

"The Virgin Mary?"

"That's right."

My heart beat like a hammer, but I decided to play it cool. Casually, I changed the subject.

"Why don't you just go back to Harbortown? Your family *needs* you in Harbortown. It's the logical place for you."

"In Legacy Oaks? Where they all bought those houses? You think that's where I belong? I should buy a house like everybody else and live there 'til I die?"

She didn't say it with attitude, but it took me by surprise.

"Is there anything wrong with that?" I countered. "After all, that's *you*, Blue. Not that I can pretend to know *you* better than you know yourself. But I can't imagine you living anywhere else. You *love* everybody in Harbortown. *You love Harbortown!* You had the most fabulous life, I thought. Was I imagining it?"

"I do love Harbortown."

"And your friends and family?"

"I love them, too."

"Then what the hell's going on?"

Looking stricken, she removed her feet from the ottoman and gazed about the room, taking in the high ceiling, faded yellow curtains, heavy pinewood desk, and the book-crammed dusty shelves. "Nothing," she said, shaking her head. "This has nothing to do with them."

"Is it because you can't go back to your old house? You don't wanna go back to Harbortown 'cause you can't live in your old house overlooking the beach?"

"The days of living there are gone."

Blue's red brick house overlooking the Mississippi beach-front highway was no longer considered habitable. She'd been visiting her sick brother in Jeremiah, a six-hour drive from Harbortown, when the monster hurricane blasted the Coast on August 29, 2005. The thirty-foot high surge of the mightiest storm on record wiped away nearly everything along the beachfront, destroying the mansions that had existed for generations, leaving nothing but a few front steps.

I'd long ago left Harbortown, having fallen in love with

7

the Big Easy, only seventy-five miles to the west. But practically all my family still lived in Harbortown, along the beach-front Highway 90. That included my older brother who, following our parents' deaths, took over our childhood home, and my younger brother who'd built a home a few miles away from him. Blue still lived in the brick house where Uncle Imad first brought her, but now alone since his death twenty-six years ago. Her step-kids had grown up and were occupying their own houses, as were our cousin, Meredith, and her grown kids and a dozen other relatives. (Sally Ann's older sister had married and moved to Dallas, Texas. Meredith's twin brother died of a heart attack quite a few years earlier.)

Later, my brothers took me to see the devastation. Mile after mile, the most gorgeous homes you'll ever see in your life were washed away in seconds, except for mine and Blue's. Built on the most elevated part of the beachfront, mine stood on Corinthian columns, the upper levels still intact, but most of the first floor washed away. FEMA later imploded the structure as my brother and sister-in-law looked on, grief-stricken and horrified. Three generations had lived in that house. At one point, my *Sitty*—my grand-mother—lived there with Uncle Imad, my parents, and all six of us kids, all under one roof. It was like a human being died that day. As for Blue's, it remained standing, a miracle rising out of the mile upon mile of ruin.

Amazingly, Blue's house sustained little damage. But as the years drifted by and nothing was done to repair it, the structure steadily eroded. It stood empty all those years because nobody could figure out what to do with it. If Blue were to move back in, she'd have to pay $25,000 a year in insurance premiums. Such an exorbitant rate hike was way beyond her means, as it was for most Gulf Coast property owners. And none but the bravest dared return to an area prone to catastrophic storms, not to mention the ever-rising crime. It surely was no place for an old woman. While my other relatives bought smaller houses in protected subdivisions farther inland, Blue remained in the Mississippi Delta 'til they could figure out what to do with her house.

"Well, I know you can't go back to your old house," I protested, "but why not live in Legacy Oaks, close to Sally Ann and Frankie? Everybody seems happy enough. I mean, considering what they've lost—their homes, their possessions—they seem amazingly well adjusted. Sally Ann and Frankie live within blocks of their girls. And Meredith's kids live on the same street. They all seem like one big happy family, visiting each other, sharing holidays. What could be more fabulous? It's the kind of life you've always loved, I thought."

She nodded dully.

"Or if not Legacy Oaks," I babbled on, "why not where my brothers live? It's great on Azalea Lane. After the storm, Hab was telling me, when the beach and Second Street and everything up to the railroad tracks looked like an atomic bomb had hit, like thousands of bombs had hit, and the looting was going on, all the men in the subdivision guarded the entrances with their hunting rifles."

It was plain she wasn't listening, not the slightest interest on her face.

"He's really made great friends," I nagged, "playing golf with them, tennis. And Mark lives within walking distance. His house has a cathedral ceiling. But if not there, how about Magnolia Street, where Meredith lives, a gated community, where everybody knows each other?"

She was gazing off in space, thumbs tapping each other.

"Blue," I said, exasperated, "why come *here*? Where you don't know a living soul but me? Who *needs* a gathering place? The Lebanese families visit with each other in their *homes.* They don't *need* a place to visit. They're wealthy. They have their country clubs and tennis clubs. Everything you're looking for is right back in Harbortown. I guess I'm not getting the picture."

Slowly, she rubbed her eyes. Grief doesn't end that quickly, but she was beginning to make me nervous.

She began staring at the silk flowers. "I expect I should be looking for a place to stay. Jamila, do you happen to have a phone book? I'd like to call the Monteleone or Royal Orleans."

"Please," I wailed, *"don't stay in a hotel.* I'd be hurt if you didn't stay with me."

"Darlin', I don't want to put you out."

"You're *not* putting me out. I'd be honored if you'd stay with me."

She thanked me. "I'll put my things away." She got up to go to the guest room and turned as she entered the hall. She looked, if not happy, at least a little relieved. "I'll rent a car so I can get around. I want to get started finding a property."

"I didn't know you still drove," I said, trotting behind her. "Blue, do you still drive?"

"A little rusty. Haven't in years. But luckily, I kept up my license." She entered the guest room, lifted a small suitcase. "So I'm in good shape."

"What property did you have in mind?" I gazed at my reflection in the bureau mirror, noting my look of bafflement.

She sat at the edge of the bed, glancing distractedly in the mirror. "Something old. And big. I'll know it when I find it."

"We'll have lunch after you unpack, then we'll go have a look around," I said. "I'll let you drive a little, so you'll get the feel of the car. And while I'm at work during the week, you can use it. I don't need it. I can walk to work, actually. It's only a twenty-minute walk. And the exercise will do me good. I'll give you an extra set of keys. You can come and go as you please."

My role as hostess was kicking in. I was enjoying the idea of her staying with me. And then I had another thought. "Did you tell Sally Ann and Meredith you were coming?"

She shook her head.

"What happens when they call Jeremiah and you're not there?"

"I have my cell, so they won't know."

Sally Ann, nine years old when Blue became her step-mom, and our cousin, Meredith, then eleven, were extremely close to Blue. But that hadn't always been the case. Shortly after Sally Ann's mom died, Uncle Imad had informed his daughter that he was bringing someone to take care of her. Sally Ann replied she didn't want anyone taking care of her. She didn't need another mother; no one could take her mother's place.

She resented Blue at first, but that didn't last long. Even-tually, they became like mother and daughter. She and Meredith would tease Blue and boss her around. As teens, they'd cuss like jailhouse thugs. I was several years younger than my cousins and picked up that vice from them, some-thing none of us ever outgrew. But Blue took it all in stride, even dishing a little back, and certainly performing all the duties a real mother would. Through the years, it became that kind of relationship in all the ways that made it real.

"Have you discussed your plans with them?"

"Not exactly." She had her back to me, holding up a summer dress. "I want to get things started before I tell them. Now, don't you say anything, Jamila."

"They're gonna raise all kinds of hell."

She reached for a pink nightie. "We'll play it by ear."

I left the room, shaking my head.

This wasn't the same woman I'd known all my life. The

11

woman I'd known was incapable of a thing like this. Blue was traditional, old-fashioned, religious. I thought her family was her whole life and she didn't give a fig about starting a business. Besides, I couldn't imagine her picking up and moving to a strange city. Maybe *Sitty*—our paternal grandmother—could start a business that could grow into a huge success, but that was another story. Blue was nothing like *Sitty* Yasmine.

I never thought of Blue in the same way. Blue was smart, energetic, creative. She was capable of succeeding at anything she did. But she'd never shown an interest in business. She'd sold real estate from time to time, but it was more a hobby, a part-time kind of thing. And after Uncle Imad brought her to Harbortown, she never even worked in the family businesses, her only passion being to raise her sister's kids.

I thought about what she'd said—the Mother of God—and wondered if maybe some cells in her brain had died. But I didn't want to think that way, so I conveniently put it aside.

~

We ate lunch at Willie Mae's Scotch House on St. Ann Street, at Blue's insistence. It was an adventurous choice. The Scotch House was a tiny shack specializing in fried chicken owned by Willie Mae Seaton, a very old Black lady in a historic part of town called Tremé. The Tremé looked like something out of a fairytale or a surreal Hawaiian village, only with pastel-colored cottages, narrow streets, and corner stores advertising spicy beans and fried fish.

A humble eatery, the Scotch House shocked the locals and gained a national rep when it won the prestigious James Beard award only months before Katrina. After getting horribly damaged by the flood waters, it was eventually rebuilt by volunteers and taken over by Willie Mae's great-granddaughter. After I'd scarfed down my red beans and rice and Blue her fried chicken, she asked me to take her on a tour of the Lower 9.

I was scared crossing the St. Claude Avenue bridge over the Industrial Canal to an area horribly decimated by the levee breach. It wasn't much of a tour. I stayed on the main road that took us past boarded businesses and flooded shotgun houses, where only a few brave souls lived amid crumbling ruin. What was it that kept them there—loyalty, economics? An insane kind of pride? I didn't give a damn, I admired them so.

The sight took my breath away. I looked over at Blue and saw death in her eyes, too. She buried her face in the newspaper, then looked up, asking if we could go on a tour of the Bywater houses. She'd seen a notice about it in the newspaper. I'd just re-crossed the bridge, and we were near that area anyway, so I asked where to get the tickets. "Bud Rip's Bar over on Piety Street," she said. We parked outside the bar, bought tickets, and walked to the first circled number on the map they gave us. We climbed the steps, entered the first house. It was an Italianate double-shotgun, built in the early twentieth century.

On the walls were bright, primitive paintings. In the dark second room with its high ceiling was a shrine with candles, sequined bottles, painted gourds, skeleton figurines, and it didn't take a rocket scientist to know this was a voodoo temple. We entered other rooms, then were ushered out back to a bare-earth alleyway. It looked like Haiti. It was utterly isolated, separated from the rest of the 'hood by a fence painted with bold images. And as we entered the rear buildings, we were stunned by the presence of thousands of voodoo dolls.

"Amazing," Blue murmured.

She was a Catholic. She attended Mass daily. But she was smiling and her eyes were bright, the opposite of disapproving.

We walked to other houses on Desire and Dauphine streets, and they were fabulous with their fluted columns, carved cornices, beaded ceilings, and flowering gardens exploding in tangled gorgeousness. There was one room in a Creole cottage I will never forget. The walls were stained golden rose, adorned with Mardi Gras Indian plumes. There were delicate candelabras and a Virgin Mary painting. It was like someone had sprinkled magic dust and put us in a trance, sending us back to an ancient time of holiness and forgotten glory. We were of the same mind, Blue and I, back in the high-ceilinged room of the innocence of our childlike longing.

We walked to the car in silence, rain drizzling on our noses. Blue had done her homework and made a list of properties from the newspaper. I let her drive. She was a little rusty, but she didn't crash into anything.

We drove first to the Warehouse District, where we looked at a 4,450-square-foot warehouse with office space and an apartment. Price: $750,000. Next, we went to the Vieux Carré to see a brick building on Dauphine with a courtyard, slave quarters, and heart-pine floors. Price: $1,500,000. I took over the wheel and, on her orders, headed for Oretha Castle Haley Boulevard, an area that long ago had been named Dryades Street.

I'd heard that by the first half of the twentieth century, Dryades was the city's largest Black commercial district as well as a working-class residential area for German, Irish, and Italian immigrants. Lots of Jews set up shop as well. Unlike Canal Street, the merchants were of many ethnicities, with African-American, Jewish, and Italian shopkeepers getting along side by side. But in the 1960s, everything changed. Now, more than forty years later, blighted buildings replaced thriving theaters, pharmacies and retail shops.

Blue watched as we drove up the wide thoroughfare to see a burnt-out school building surrounded by a chain-link fence and a homeless shelter across the street.

I stopped at a red light.

A man looking like a mummy, ashen with matted hair, stood on the neutral ground and began making his way toward us. He stood within a few feet of us, stretching out his swollen arm, silently begging for a handout. He was less than a man; he looked dead, some man's body risen from the grave, matted, gray, swollen, ghoulish. The light changed. I sped off.

We passed a vacant building with metal scraps piled atop a dilapidated overhang and windows removed to expose gutted rooms. Further on, a Black-owned art gallery with a sign reading, *For Sale by Owner*. In the next block, a corner building with the signage, *Ocean Seafood*, and a 'For Sale' sign across the entranceway.

Then we passed Terpsichore Street, and Blue's eyes lit up. Before us stood a Classic frame-style house with a two-level wood gallery and bracketed cornices, and Blue practically screamed, "*Stop here!*" We were in the heart of Central City, better known for drug deals and drive-by shootings than polite social get-togethers, but Blue had found her building.

I stopped, didn't get out.

"You don't want to stop here," I pleaded.

"Only a minute," she exulted. "A *minute!*"

"Don't you want to go to the next stop on your list?"

"I promise, Jamila, we won't be long."

We had traveled along Oretha Castle for a good six blocks, and there wasn't a soul on that street who didn't look penniless.

"I don't know why you want to do this," I grumbled, forcing myself out of the car.

We saw an orange tree in a patch of yard with plump ripe fruit, and Blue looked ecstatic. She got out of the car, ascended the steps, strolled the length of the porch, and peered through a floor-to-ceiling window. I came up behind her and looked in. It was dark inside, but I could still make out the high ceiling.

"Beautiful," Blue said breathlessly.

The front door was locked. We went around back, looking through a peephole in a wood fence. She smiled excitedly as she turned to me.

"I can plant palm trees and elephant ears, banana trees... and chrysanthemums. Maybe a couple of magnolias and crepe myrtle. I can start a grapevine. Honey, this is as good as a million-dollar French Quarter property. I bet I can get it for cheap." She glanced down at her paper. "It's advertised for $200,000. I'm going to offer $120,000."

"Chrissake, why would you want to do *that*? Anyone'd be out of their *mind* coming to this area?"

"We'll see."

It crossed my mind a second time: Blue must be losing hers.

CHAPTER 2

*A*fter Blue and I had eaten a Lebanese supper of *kibbe* and *tabouli*, we settled in my living room, I with a Bud Light, she with a glass of wine. It was getting late. I sat in the armchair across the room from her, legs stretching out on the ottoman, while Blue, head resting on pillows, lay supine across the sofa. She seemed comfortable, head reclining, hand dangling across her forehead, the other falling over the edge of the seat cushion.

"Blue," I said, "don't you think it's time to call Sally Ann?"

"I've been putting it off."

"No time like now to call your daughter." I picked up the phone. She waved her hand to stop me.

"Let's not do it right now," she said. "Tomorrow..."

"Can't you tell me what's going on?"

"You promise not to tell?"

Only the standup lamp across the room was turned on, the reflected light shining across the stereo in a corner of the room behind her head. Her eyes were half-closed. She seemed to be nodding off.

"You know," she said drowsily, not waiting for an answer,

"when you get to be almost eighty-two, you think the path ahead of you is clear. No hard decisions to make, no crossroads to stumble on. But my life has been... well, complicated. You wouldn't think so. My brothers and sisters are gone. There's no reason for me to stay in Jeremiah anymore.

"So the obvious choice," she went on, "would be for me to go home—to Harbortown. That's where I want to be. I have a wonderful family there. Sally Ann, Frankie, Meredith, everybody waiting for me. Their children, children's children... babies to play with..." She was on the verge of drifting off, but her sleepy voice droned on. "Kathy and Bashir... their children. Your brothers... their families. A full life waiting. I could live with Sally Ann or find a place of my own. Resume the prayer group. Play the organ at Mass. My regular bridge game with my friends. Sell real estate from time to time. The Revelers' balls, something to look forward to..."

Her reveries would soon be over, I thought, but her sluggish voice continued on.

"... My friend, Flora Mae... we did everything together. And I truly, truly miss her." Her aching loneliness could be heard. She seemed fragile in the reflected lamp light.

She sat up, drank more wine, and lay back down on the sofa. "After my brother's funeral, I began packing my things to go. Sally Ann was waiting for me to call to tell her when I was ready to leave Jeremiah so she could drive me back to Harbortown. One evening, several weeks after the funeral, I'd almost finished packing, and I remember lying in bed feeling alone in that terrible room, feeling sorry for myself, going over all the happy times I'd shared with my brothers and sisters and cousins..." She said each name with loving tenderness, tears welling in her eyes.

"There were ghosts in that room. I was the only surviving one. It's hard letting go. I started thinking about my married

18

life in Harbortown and how Imad was gone and your daddy and mama..."

She wiped her eyes, struggling to keep her voice from wavering. "I fell into a state of mourning, the deepest, darkest hole. My life was about death. I was surrounded by it. And then"—her voice lifted—"Mother Mary came to me."

A car passed outside. There was the distant wailing of a baby. From out of nowhere came the patter of rain, more and more urgently 'til it completely surrounded the room.

"I know it sounds strange, honey. I wouldn't be here on my own. This is what was *given* to me. This is where Mary wants me to be."

I tightened my fingers around my can. "You said that before... Mary."

"A voice."

"I see."

She peered at me from the corner of her eye.

"Maybe it was only grief," I reflected, "making you hear things..."

She glanced at the desk, roused herself, sat in the middle of the sofa, and crossed her legs. "No, darlin', it was Mary. I don't know how to explain it. But when Mother Mary speaks, you never ever forget. You never have the slightest doubt. And from that moment on, I may not have known what She wanted of me, but I knew I had to obey Her."

A car splashed outside, racing through the built-up rainwater, and more cars and more rain. She was alert to it. A calming, almost stupefied presence radiated from her, but she was aware of where she was.

"And what did Mary say?" I asked.

"'Go to New Orleans. Make a gathering place. Be there to welcome them for me.' No vision, no apparition, nothing even close to that. It wasn't like Lourdes or Medjugorje or Fatima. But there was no question it was Her."

"But how do you *know*?"

Blue shrugged. She placed an elbow against her crossed knee. Her chin rested in the palm of her hand, the long day taking its toll. I can tell when someone has been through grief; it's plastered all over the face, at least inside the eyes. And it was finding its home in hers. She looked up, wanting me to believe.

"She came *three times*," she said, raising her voice. "Each night when I'd go to bed, I'd lie there waiting, hoping for Her presence. And just when I was about to doze off, that's when I'd hear the voice. Saying the same thing, three nights in a row: 'Go to New Orleans. Make a gathering place. Be there to welcome them for me.'"

Her tone was intense; she was almost begging me to believe. "It wasn't a hallucination or my imagination since it happened three times that way."

"Uh-huh."

She waited.

I shook my head. "Blue, I don't even know what to say."

She leaned in, *"I don't either. I don't. All I know is it was Her! Mary's voice*—of that much I am sure. It was loving and comforting and beautiful. And there was nothing to be afraid of. It put me at ease. It was not of this world. And there is no explaining to anyone who hasn't heard."

She said it with such passion, you could almost be convinced.

"I am sure and will never doubt it."

I couldn't hear the rain anymore, only water rushing down a gutter pipe, an occasional car splashing through the street.

She sat up, staring at her empty glass. "So what does one do when one hears the voice of Mary? I tried to understand what it was She wanted. I prayed She'd give me some direction. But that direction never came. So I tried filling in the parts. 'Go to New Orleans.' That much was clear. 'Make a gathering place.' She wanted me to prepare a place where people would come. Most of the people I know are Lebanese. So I assumed it was the Lebanese She wanted me to gather. And what to do with them? I had no idea. My holiday celebrations were my only experience at getting people together —the New Year's Eve parties. Do you remember my New Year's Eve parties?"

Every so often, I'll play a video cassette that Blue put together and gave to me years ago. It captures the moments of our families' lives as, from 1965 through 1987, they danced and celebrated and masqueraded and preened while a thrill of joy rushed through me watching their antics to the strains of *At Last* or *Don't Sit Under the Apple Tree.*

In amazement, I'd watch: a baby tottering in the grass; nine-year-old Sally Ann dancing; my brothers kicking a ball; Meredith and her twin, Michael, at their Catholic Confirmation; my brother sticking his tongue out at the camera; Meredith pirouetting in ballet slippers; my mom radiant and young, with long, dark flashing lashes, the innocence in her eyes, as she smiled in her winter coat, coquettishly throwing a snowball. Or another scene in which she stood in front of our circular entrance garden, the blazing azaleas red and rose and pink, our great towering mansion magnificent in the background.

There were hundreds of images leading up to the best: Blue's famous New Year's Eve parties.

Each year, it was an elegant affair, bringing every Lebanese together. My mother's sister and her husband, who happens to be my daddy's nephew, would drive down from Mobile, Alabama, in a station wagon packed with seven kids. Blue's siblings and cousins would come from the Mississippi Delta. Sally Ann's older sister and her family from Dallas, along with another relative's family from Jackson, Mississippi; another aunt—widowed—with her brood of ten, all grown and spread out all over the Deep South; and my mother's brother, a World War II hero, as handsome as an *Esquire* model, flying to be with us from Greensboro, North Carolina.

It was like a Hollywood premiere.

They'd crowd together in every room of Blue's and Uncle Imad's house, holding cocktails and plates of food, the men in dark suits, women wearing flowers picked from Blue's garden, Sally Ann with her curly hair, me in my pigtails, Uncle Imad smoking a cigar, a stunningly beautiful Blue.

Or they'd crowd around the banquet table with its tall candles and centerpiece topped with a ripe pineapple. And there'd be massive amounts of food cooked by Blue herself: *kibbe, mihshi malfouf, babaghanooj, hoummus b'tahini, sambousik, fa'toy'yeh b'sbaanegh, djaaj mishwi, laham mishwi, tabouli*, and the most delicious sweets: date walnut delights, *k'naafeh* pastries, *b'learwa*, and *ma'mool*. Blue would spend weeks cooking before storing everything in a huge freezer in her walk-in kitchen pantry in preparation for the great night.

Watching that video brought back so many memories: My older brother, a teen then, getting drunk on Jack Daniels, talking out of his head on the bed in our cousin's back room; me running around the house raising all kinds of hell with my cousins 'til some grownup would put a stop to it. And afterwards—after we'd leave at three in the morning and walk the twenty yards or so next door to my house and gossip in bed all night with my girl cousins and get up at dawn and go to New Year's Mass, then pile into cars, my relatives and family, and drive the hour and a half to New Orleans to watch the Sugar Bowl football game, freezing, exhausted, in that outdoor stadium, then attend another cousin's party then drive back home again—after all these memories would come the knowledge that most of these people were dead already. And these were the people I loved, ghosts singing sweetly to the music in the background, *"Georgia... sweet Georgia... just an old sweet song..."*

Blue didn't wait for a reply. She forged straight ahead: "Well, I had to do what Mother Mary told me, that much was crystal clear. And I had to have faith that if I did the best I could, more would be revealed to me. This is the most amazing thing I've ever done. But I'm Hers. And this I know for sure: She will never abandon me."

Her face was illuminated, the strain and worry gone. The rain ceased, the only sound now being the dull humming of the computer. I got up, walked to the kitchen, and brought back the bottle of wine. I saw she truly believed.

It reminded me of something that happened when I was eight. I vaguely recalled that morning when my mother, Blue, and I were at some place that could only have been a convent. I remembered it being dark, and the smell of incense filling my nostrils and going down a long hall with nuns in black robes, then sticking my finger in a font and crossing myself, and it was so holy. It felt mystical and hazy. But, like a vivid dream, I remembered the afternoon. I was walking in Blue's side yard, as big as a football field, that stretched from Second Street all the way to the beachfront highway. And I was in my short-shorts and cotton top, heading toward the beach highway.

It was a beautiful summer day, windy, the sea breeze rippling the branches of the live oaks. I was walking toward the grey-green waters of the Mississippi Sound against the strength of a cooling wind when an incredible feeling came over me. I could hear the gorgeous wind music, feel emotions so powerful I knew I'd have to capture them in words, resurrect the splendor of the moment, for I'd never feel them again. I knew that. Knew nothing would ever again be as powerful, not on this earth. And the words that came to me were peace and joy and love, only magnified a thousand times from what I'd ever known. A fleeting glimpse of heaven.

So I could swallow what she told me. It didn't matter anyway, whether it was the voice of Mary or something she'd imagined. Blue was no more capable of walking away from what she *thought* she heard than from her duty to her sister's kids.

She told me something years ago when I was sitting on her kitchen stool, eating stuffed grape leaves from a china saucer. In those days, we whiled away the summers that way, when school was out, and we were reminiscing about the day she first moved to Harbortown after marrying Uncle Imad. She told me, "Nobody marries their sister's husband. It's just not done. But my mother told me those children needed me. And I knew that it was true. And so I accepted his proposal."

It was not in her genes to turn away from duty. She never took the easy way. Once in grammar school, I showed her a bonus question in math. I asked if she could help me. The next morning, before I left for school, Blue called me over. She'd figured out the answer, staying up all night. It was something I'll never forget, though I don't know why it should surprise me. *She never gives up.* And she never gets tired.

In the years following Uncle Imad's death, when her step kids moved out to start their own families and Blue was alone in her brick house, and my older brother and his family had taken over my childhood home, my brother would speak fondly of her. Blue would be gone morning, noon and night, he'd joked, tooling around with pals, doing all kinds of charity work, visiting family in the evenings.

Even when I was young, she had more energy than I. Once, she and I visited a cathedral in Biloxi to support my cousin MaryLynn A-Baki, a singer. MaryLynn was rehearsing for a solo performance in a big Christmas concert. Afterwards, when every cell in my body yearned to get some rest, Blue begged me to accompany her somewhere else. I think it was to a museum. I simply stood in awe of her.

And now, years later, in the late spring of 2009, here she was at my house. She poured herself more wine. I popped another top. We talked late into the night, rehashing old memories. I'd always loved hearing the stories of our families' adventure during Hurricane Camille. I was away when the storm hit the Mississippi Coast in '69, and my family went over to Blue's to ride it out, so that 19 relatives and friends hovered together that scary night, from a one-year-old infant to my 105-year-old *Sitty*. They trembled in terror through the howling dark, as the waters rose to 23-feet above sea level and a hundred tornadoes hovered within Camille. Blue told me she trembled as the winds sounded like sledgehammers against the walls of her house. Like thrill seekers craving ghost stories, Blue and I craved storm stories. Little could we have imagined that 36 years after Camille would come the monster of them all, Katrina.

~

*N*ext morning, I left for work, leaving Blue my old Ford Taurus. When I got home after five, the phone started ringing. There was shouting in the background. It was Blue, begging me: *"Come over."*

"Where?"

"To the building on Oretha Castle. I bought it."

Holy bananas in chocolate syrup.

"I gave them a down payment," she yelled into the phone.

"And what's that noise in the background?" I asked.

"Meredith and Sally Ann." She sounded panic-stricken. "Could you *please* come over?"

I hurried to find my keys before remembering Blue had my car. The phone rang a second time. "I just remembered..." —Blue's voice, shrill—"I have your car. We'll come get you."

"No, I'll ride my bike."

"Okay." She hung up.

I hadn't ridden my bike in years, but I mounted it anyway. Riding down Euterpe Street, I passed five vacant tenement buildings with black crosses spray-painted on each one, the markings of the first responders in the days following Katrina. Across the street from burgeoning weeds, on the front porches lay bags of trash, ratty sofas, and dust-covered washers. Windows boarded up, rain-soaked rugs littering the yard. It felt creepy riding through a slum without a living soul, spooky to imagine what it'd be like stranded there at night. In the four years since the levee failures flooded the Big Easy, not one person on Euterpe Street appeared to have come back. I felt relief riding out of there and entering Oretha Castle.

They were standing on the hot pavement, worry in my cousins' eyes, anxiety in Blue's. I dismounted, pretending I hadn't noticed, and hugged Meredith and Sally Ann, catching a glimpse of Blue's gratitude in my peripheral vision.

"Come on, darlins," Blue said, hurrying us, "I'm taking us on a tour."

CHAPTER 3

$\mathcal{Y}$ears ago, when I was a girl, I'd hear my mother nagging my father for it seemed like ages to remodel our run-down house. After the renovations were complete, the rough beauty of the place, the cracked walls and peeling paint, had been transformed into stunning elegance. The interior of Blue's building reminded me of my childhood home before the renovations. The building was gutted and stripped of all furniture, yet one could feel its peacefulness, massiveness, and old-world charm. It boasted double full-length windows, tall cedar doors grained to resemble mahogany, and beaded ceiling beams.

Blue was busy talking.

"Over here will be the bar... and here will be the stage for the band... and here will be the dance floor... and here will be the kitchen. And the *shusma*—bathroom—will be over here... and here will be a small personal space... and here will be the eating booths. We'll knock down this wall, so it'll be one big room. And, darlins', come over here. Let me show you this beautiful winding staircase. Mahogany, look at that..."

"Blue, can we talk?" Meredith interrupted.

My cousin, Meredith, tall and slender, with great dark, piercing eyes, took after the no-nonsense Salhany side of her family—her daddy, Walid's—not the appeasing, conciliatory Hamieh side. And though she could be gracious with guests, with those she truly loved she was as brutally honest as a federal prosecutor. Having known her all my life, I knew that beneath the toughness and crassness beat the heart of a caring person. I also knew Blue was in for a rough ride.

"Have you lost your *mind?*" Sally Ann chimed in. "*Jesus Christ*, what are we *doing* here?"

Ever since she was a child, Sally Ann had been short and chubby, with short-cropped curly hair. I can remember her standing in her slip on a bathroom scale with Uncle Imad hovering over her, scolding her if she hadn't followed the diet he'd imposed. I think, over the years, she must have resented Uncle Imad's intrusiveness, for she grew heavier with time, a rebellion against her father. But in recent months, she'd had gastric bypass surgery, and I was shocked to see how thin she was.

"Blue," Sally Ann bellowed, "we need to talk about what you're *doing.*"

"Darlin', let me finish showing you 'round first." Blue hustled us along. "And then we can go have a drink somewhere."

"Nobody wants a drink," said Meredith. "You need to clue us in on what you're *doing.*"

Blue led us up the winding staircase, talking breathlessly as she went along, saying, "C'mon, gals, let's put some pepper in your step," bouncing, pretending everything was hunky-dory, swinging arms, in perilous disregard for the precipitous, shadowy ascent, the loose and missing boards. My cousins and I struggled to see in the dark, clinging to the rail.

When we finally reached the upstairs landing, Blue's enthusiasm bubbled over.

"Look here, this will be the guestroom... and there'll be another room across the hall. Here will be the living quarters... And my bedroom will be over here. There'll be two *shusmas*—two bathrooms. And this is where the sauna'll be. Come look at the gallery."

Exuberantly, she led us to the second-floor gallery, raising the floor-to-ceiling window and stepping out. Before us, to our right and left, stood a vista of shuttered buildings on a street that once upon a time had strutted and gleamed with life.

Meredith's eyes were ablaze. Sally Ann's mouth dropped open. The top of the orange tree towered above the wooden balustrade, and a few overripe oranges rotted on the gallery floor. I gazed at the vast thoroughfare, desolate and lonely except for a few stragglers, and it made me wonder what pivotal event had brought about its demise. But Blue was thinking other thoughts.

"One day there'll be folks filling the streets again..." She peered dreamily to her left, toward the Quarter, and to her right, Uptown. "There'll be festivals and parades and Christmas shopping and Hanukkah shopping. Honey, can't you just picture this street bursting with life? It only takes one person to get things started, darlin'. You know, I did my homework. Once, merchants did a thriving business here, long before you were born."

I was trying to recall whether Jews shopped for Hanukkah and whether the Jewish merchants set Hanukkah candle stands in their display windows and lit candles and read the story of the Maccabees when a mild breeze blew past me. The light had begun to fade. I worried we should be getting home. A flurry of activity. I looked down and saw a stranger.

He was stealing my bike.

"Hey, don't *do* that!" I yelled at the top of my lungs. "*Stop or I'm calling the cops!*"

I rushed to the stairwell, trying to hustle down, treading carefully at the same time because I didn't want to fall. And when I finally reached the street, there was this punk grinning broadly, riding into the sunset with me shouting after him, "*Hey, you can't get away with this—*"

But he didn't give a damn. He vanished into Euterpe Street, where I wasn't about to go. I decided not to call the cops, though I'd threatened to do so. The city was short on cops, and I figured, even if I reported it, they probably wouldn't show up. As I turned to go back inside, I heard a commotion coming from the staircase.

"Blue, don't get up!" It was Meredith's panicked voice. "*We've got you. We've got you.*"

Sally Ann: "Don't move. We've got you!"

Halfway up the stairs, Blue was lying face up, my cousins above and below her, Meredith holding onto her feet, Sally Ann hanging on to what she could, Blue favoring her left arm as they tried to keep her from sliding down. We made sure her legs weren't hurt and that there was nothing wrong with the other arm, before clumsily, arduously guiding her down the flight of stairs.

～

"*B*lue, this is *bullshit!*" Meredith glowered over her gin fizz.

Blue was drinking a stinger, and Sally Ann and I, champagne, celebrating our great fortune at having barely averted a catastrophe. We had loaded Blue into Meredith's Mercedes and taken her to Touro Infirmary. She'd stayed in the ER for hours before they finally took the

X-rays. And that's when we got the news: She hadn't broken anything. It was only a muscle strain. We headed for the bar at the Column's Hotel.

It was half past nine at night. The moon hung low as we walked under a gigantic oak tree whose gnarled branches stretched across streetcar tracks high above St. Charles Avenue. We entered the Victorian Lounge of the 126-year-old Italianate mansion that had been a popular hotel/bar for years. Since it was summer, the lounge was practically empty, except for a few college kids hanging out at the bar. We sat in a corner booth.

"What's gotten into you?" Meredith exploded. "Don't you know you're an old lady? You'll *die* before you get one penny of your investment back. Uncle Imad's turning in his grave. Blue, don't you see what kind of street that is? Someone's gonna get killed. *Unbelievable. Unbelievable*—you bought that rundown scuzzy building."

"Mama Mia, take it easy! You'll liveaah longer!" Blue laughed.

It was a favorite saying of Uncle Imad's whenever anyone got mad. 'Til now, it had always defused the tension.

"Blue, this is plain stupid." It was Meredith's favorite saying.

"It's not funny." Sally Ann jutted out her bottom lip. "You nearly broke your goddamn neck."

Blue threw her shoulders back. She'd offered $120,000, she said proudly, and that had been accepted, and she was thrilled and deeply grateful to have got the price down from $200,000. And she was going to draw up the plans herself and hire Mexicans to do the work. That would save a lot of money. And she was going to apply for loans and grants, and anyone who knew the rich history of the neighborhood knew what a find she had. Then she started telling us its story, putting her best spin on everything.

Oretha Castle Haley Boulevard had been a racially mixed, thriving business district back in the 1830s. By the 1940s, there were more than 200 businesses. Some of the merchants on Canal, the city's main commercial corridor, didn't like Blacks trying on the clothes.

"But, honey," Blue noted cheerfully, "everybody was treated equally back when Oretha Castle was named Dryades Street. At that time, the Blacks owned clothing shops and pool halls and insurance companies, everything you could possibly imagine, so folks could go shopping and eat lunch, then come back later to have supper.

"And there were all these restaurants," she regaled us, "including Dorsey Franklin's in the 400 block that specialized in Creole food. And there was Dejoie's Pharmacy in the 1800 block that had an ice-cream parlor kids loved. And there were *Yahoud*—Jews—from Russia. They opened supermarkets and furniture stores, and a delicatessen that served kosher pickles. There was no closing hour. They stayed open 'til way late—'til all the customers left. It was lovely... absolutely *lovely*... 'til all the merchants began to leave."

"Why did they?" Sally Ann wanted to know, getting caught up in the story.

"It went downhill in the 60s." Blue finished off her stinger. "Before that, Dryades was the only street where Blacks could shop without being treated poorly. And then in the '60s, after the civil rights movement, other areas began to integrate, and so that was where the Black shoppers went. That's also when the Whites began moving to the suburbs."

"How do *you* know?" Meredith glowered.

"Why, honey, I did my homework."

"So you've just bought a building on a street nobody goes to, where the sidewalks are broken and the potholes big as swimming pools and there's stealing going on and Lord knows what else. And you bought it in the middle of a worldwide recession. Nice thinking, Blue." Meredith grabbed her Gucci bag and stampeded toward the bar. We saw her bumming cigarettes from a stranger.

"Put that down!" Sally Ann demanded.

"I will *not...*"

Meredith had slipped back into our booth, crossing her legs and puffing furiously. "I'm worried about your mental health." Her eyes fixed on Blue. *"Seriously."* She took another drag. "What has gotten into you?"

It was the eight-hundred-pound gorilla in the room. A fine time for an explanation, not that my cousins would have bought it, but the occasion definitely called for one. If I'd been Blue, I'd have caved in and spilled my guts about the Virgin Mary and all. Instead, head down, in a tone as earnest as she could make it, sounding for all the world as if she believed it and would go to her grave believing it without a moment's hesitation, Blue said: "This corridor will bounce back."

She let that hang in the air. And then, "And I'll be there to see it."

She leaned in, going for the kill: "Did you see the Frederick Douglass Cultural Center across the street?"

I, for one, hadn't. My feet had barely touched the gallery floor when the great bike heist took place.

"It's open," Blue said, "and operating. They put on exhibits so Black artists can sell their art. And they give theater performances, seminars and lectures focusing on the Black community. And one block down is Café Master Chef. That's where at-risk kids work. They learn skills so they can get jobs in the restaurant industry. A Jesuit priest started it. And there's the Jacob Lawrence Gallery and the James Earl Jones Theater, in the next block going Uptown. Did you see that three-story schoolhouse with the red masonry façade? It was built in 1910. Honey, that was

Myrtle Banks Elementary 'til they closed it a couple years ago. Later, it caught fire. They're making it a Civil Rights museum."

"*How-de-do*, you missed your *calling*," Meredith said sarcastically. "You outta work for the Chamber of Commerce, Blue. Now, let me get this straight. Correct me if I'm wrong. You're opening a bar or café—whatever you prefer to call it—for Lebanese on an *abeid* street?" She shook her head and, in a tone so scornful, I couldn't even look at Blue, she said: "This goes *beyond* stupid. *Lunacy* is what I'd call it."

You couldn't exactly call *abeid* a slur. It was an Arabic word for Black people. Still, the way she said it sounded so mean that I had to ask her what she meant by that.

"There's nothing racist about what I said," she said, throwing daggers at me with her eyes. "Any Lebanese would be *proud* to come to a street where Black people lived as long as they kept it up. But they'd be *crazy* to come to a street where *nobody* lived—where most of the buildings are boarded up."

"Now, let me put it another way," Meredith continued with her explanation. She lit a cigarette off the end of her old one. "I don't care if they're Black or White or any color of the living rainbow as long as they don't hurt us. But you know as well as I, there's not a soul walking that street that isn't a drunk or thief or homeless person." Blowing smoke in my face, she grabbed her purse and wandered off.

Another silence hung in the air 'til Meredith came back to start another fight, saying it wasn't too late, Blue could still get her down payment back. How much was it? Forty thousand? There was still time—she could get out of this.

Yet Blue, unwavering and persistent, would not give in. And Sally Ann was nagging Meredith to death to stamp out that filthy cigarette. Didn't she remember what they'd found on her last chest X-ray? And it was my cousins who gave in, and we all got drunk.

~

*N*ext morning, Blue asked me to drop her off at the building. We bickered. I insisted she take my car in case something terrible happened and she needed to get away, but she quickly nixed that idea. I needed it for work, she said, then she instructed me to meet her after work. Worn down, I let her have her way.

After dropping her off, I obsessed. She might fall down the stairs again with nobody around to help, or some drifter might wander in and grab her purse and beat her up. My thoughts turned even darker, with someone raping her and slitting her throat and slicing her up and cooking her body parts, things that had really happened in this city and been headline news in the local paper. By noon, I left the office.

It was blistering hot, even for late May, as I drove up Oretha Castle and saw Blue in the rippling heat trekking down the steaming sidewalk. She was headed in the direction of the fenced-in, burnt-out schoolhouse, a solitary figure on one side of the street while, on the other, homeless people lined up outside the Baptist Mission.

"Hey, what's up?" I said, slowing down.

She was on her way to the big church near Calliope, she said, to ask a priest if he knew of any laborers.

"Get in," I said, stopping. "We'll go to my church. There's a wonderful pastor there. They've just started a Spanish-speaking Mass. Father Tony might know of some laborers."

Standing under the stinging sun, Blue, dressed in golfing clothes, hair damp around her brow, got out her hanky. And that's when I saw her purse.

"Blue, *never* walk the street with a purse, not 'less you're in some mall in Old Metairie. You'll get *robbed*." In recent years, I'd been mugged three times.

We parked on North Rampart Street and entered Our Lady of Guadalupe. Father Tony, from a large Sicilian family in upstate New York, knew of someone to recommend. He told us Latinos had poured into the city looking for work after the storm. There'd been estimates of up to 60,000 illegals still living in the Crescent City. They were hard workers, Father told us, but I already knew that. They'd not only rebuilt our devastated city but the even worse-off Mississippi Coast, literally saving Harbortown. Now, four years after the storm, many were sitting idle, desperate for work, after the construction business took a dive.

"I know just the right person—Alejandro Cruz," he said enthusiastically. "There was a fire in the church six months ago. We caught it early, thank God, and it didn't do much damage. Alejandro was the man who did the repairs. I'll call him."

He reached for the phone. Blue stopped him.

"Does he speak English, Father? We don't speak Spanish."

"He speaks excellent English."

"Then, please, that would be a help."

Father Tony spoke in Spanish before handing Blue the phone. She asked in English if he could meet her at the building. It was agreed, and we left.

❧

*R*elief shone in Blue's eyes as we drove back to the building, stopping only once to pick up sandwiches. Alejandro got there first. He was seated behind the wheel of a beat-up Jeep Cherokee, with two men seated in the back. When he got out, he was a bruiser of a man, thick and broad and barrel-chested, with the most brooding

36

expression, cinnamon skin, and raven hair falling past his shoulders. His eyes bore into us. He looked intimidating—imposing—and I could only guess how he looked to Blue, like some big Mexican drug dealer.

It would take a while to get to know him because Alejandro was very reserved. Later, I was to discover he was a gentle man, a man of kindness and integrity. He was an oil painter who supported himself through construction work. He'd gone to college in Mexico City to study art. In his spare time, he worked as a street artist at Jackson Square in the Quarter.

He offered Blue his hand. He introduced us to Evandro Paiva and Otavio Vieiva, skilled tradesmen from Brazil. He spoke to them in Portuguese. We followed Blue up the porch steps. She unlocked the door, letting the men in first. They paused to take a look around. Blue showed Alejandro a rough floor plan she'd sketched. She told him what she wanted, and it was agreed she'd pay him and his men $2,000 a week plus materials.

The work would begin next morning, knocking down walls, tearing down the center wall that divided the front room into halves. They shook on it and were about to leave. We headed for the door. Blue got there first. She reached to open the door, but it swung open on its own.

Standing before us were Meredith and Sally Ann.

CHAPTER 4

*B*ehind Meredith and Sally Ann stood the men of the family: Elie and Frankie.

And behind them, a stranger.

The stranger behind my cousins wore a starched, long-sleeved white shirt, buttoned at the neck and wrists. He had thin lips, a narrow nose, and a defined jaw and forehead. He appeared to be in his mid-fifties. He stood several paces behind my cousins, but his curious eyes bore into Blue. It was fascinating the way he seemed to will himself into anonymity, melting into the gathering, silent and aloof, but at the same time, he couldn't keep his eyes off Blue.

Blue took in our family, giving the stranger a once-over.

Suddenly, Alejandro's hand moved toward his pocket, his eyes sparkling with anger (or so it appeared to us, strangers who didn't know him) as he moved to pull out a silver object.

At that moment, Frankie's hand went down as well—automatically, instinctively—and I realized he was reaching for a gun. Alejandro, a distance behind and to the right of Blue, froze. Blue threw up her hands.

"*Wakkif... wakkif... stop...*" She stretched out her hand to Frankie.

Elie moved toward Frankie, Evandro and Otavia toward Alejandro.

And then, nobody moved.

In the stunning realization of what he'd almost done, Frankie halted, his hand balled into a fist, and it stayed that way, suspended, slightly above his waistband. Frankie—Sally Ann's husband—had in recent years become a cop. He'd owned a women's dress factory in Harbortown, started by his father, but when the old man passed away, Frankie liquidated the business and went into the kind of work that was more his type of thing: He became a liaison between the Harbortown police and the FBI, working in the area of insurance fraud after the storm, later on cases involving child porn.

"Stop!" Blue pleaded.

She rushed toward Frankie and grabbed his wrist, her body positioned between him and Alejandro.

The men fixed on each other, Frankie on Alejandro, Elie on the Brazilian workers. Elie—Sally Ann's brother—looked like a Marine braced for war. He had always been my good buddy, though he and I were years apart. As a teen, I'd give him back rubs, and sometimes when he was away, I'd hop over to Blue's house and head for his room to sit for hours gawking at the pictures in his *Playboy* magazines while Blue sewed in the next room. Elie worked beside his father—my Uncle Imad—in their men's store. But he was retired now, having worked hard, living a bachelor's life in Harbortown.

"I'm telling you, honey, there is no need for this!"

Blue's voice quavered. Her breath came in ragged jags. She reached over and hugged Frankie before stepping back and embracing Alejandro, whom we now could see had been reaching for his cell phone. Blue put an arm through his. It was an instinctive gesture, intended to quell the storm, to show we were all family. And, amazingly, it worked. Frankie stood mortified, ears turning bright red. But Alejandro's unforgiving eyes stayed stuck on him like daggers.

"I do not appreciate what you do," Alejandro drew himself up. "My friend, you have no right to pull a gun." He turned to look behind him, protectively, at Evandro and Otavio.

He waited.

"I *didn't.*" Frankie blushed. "And who, may I ask, are you?"

"You almost did. So dangerous... *ridiculous.*" Alejandro wouldn't let it go. "We were going to die from your foolishness..."

"Frankie, this is Alejandro Cruz." Blue slipped her arm from out of Alejandro's and draped it protectively around his back. "And this is his flooring-and-tile specialist, Evandro Paira, and his master carpenter, Otavio Vieiva. *Hinni ashabna*, Frankie—*they are our friends.*"

"Honey..." Blue quickly added, catching her breath. "... what on earth are y'all doing here?"

"We've come to take you home," Frankie said. "I thought we'd have lunch at Mandina's first, then get your things and head home."

Blue lowered her head. The temperature was hovering well above one hundred degrees inside, and the stranger behind my cousins took out a hanky to wipe his face. Blue looked up and saw him.

"Who are you?" Blue asked politely.

A dark stain appeared under the stranger's arm as he nervously patted his brow. "I'm Chester Watson," he declared formally, putting away the hanky before pinching the bridge of his sweaty nose.

Blue looked confused. She waited for an explanation. Her mouth opened wide and then surprise lit up her eyes. "Aren't you Stanley Watson's child?"

She waited for an acknowledgment, but the stranger never answered.

"You're a doctor?" she stammered. "I heard you were a doctor... isn't that what your daddy told me? Yes... yes... that's what Stanley told me..."

"A geriatric psychiatrist," Meredith said, enunciating every syllable.

It was heartbreaking to watch the look on Blue's face. And this was the fascinating part: Blue was from a generation that never acknowledged humiliation. The more mortifying a situation, the less likely she was to acknowledge it (my daddy was that way, never revealing what he really knew). And instead of doing what a younger person might, which might be to cuss out the offender or slam the door in his face, Blue put on her best hospitality voice, which made it even sadder, because we all knew what she recognized.

"Honey, a pleasure to meet you."

Shuddering, girding herself, there was an instant when it looked like she might crawl into some dark corner. Instead, she drew herself up, as if casting off all self-doubt, literally shaking it off her shoulders, and strutted away to retrieve her legal pad. She returned and, with strained dignity, handed the pad to Frankie.

"Here," she said, "I'd like you to see my drawings." To Alejandro: "Tomorrow we'll tear down the center wall." Anxiously adding, "I'll see you tomorrow, Alejandro? Tomorrow at nine?"

"Wait," Frankie drew closer, "you're coming home with us."

"*No...*"

Elie moved toward Blue. "Do you realize what you're doing? You've never renovated a building in your life. You can't possibly know the headaches."

Alejandro took something out of his pocket, carefully this

time, and handed it to Frankie. It was a business card. He explained his qualifications and asked if they might need references. He jotted down names and phone numbers and tried handing that to him, too.

"Blue," Frankie said, turning away from him, "we have a responsibility not to let you do this. Renovating a building's exhausting work. And what the hell for? If you want to start a business, we can start one in Harbortown. Elie's got plenty of property. You can occupy one of his buildings. And we'll have someone run it for you. But you can't stay here on your own."

"I'm *not* here on my own," Blue cried, and that was when she turned to me.

They must have thought she was trying to tell them that I would take care of her, but I knew she had someone higher in mind, someone of the heavenly sort.

She turned back to Frankie. "Now, don't you worry, darlin'. You go back home now, you hear? I'll see you real soon, I promise."

Elie's hand was on Blue's back, hustling her to the door, Meredith on one side of her and Sally Ann on the other. Too soon, she was on the porch, Frankie in front of her, Elie in back, Meredith and Sally Ann taking her elbows to guide her down the steps. Taking his clue from them, Chester Watson, the stranger, rushed back down to the street below and, after Frankie tossed him the key, he dutifully held open the car door.

"*No!*" Blue howled.

But no one was listening.

Maybe they could have got her in the car that way, pushing forcefully like the mighty ocean, except a cop happened to be leaving the Frederick Douglass Center and making his way across the street. He stood on the sidewalk, glaring at them before demanding to know what was going on.

"Nothing, officer," Elie said in his most mellifluous voice, all overripe Southern charm. "We were just bringing my stepmom home. To Harbortown, where she lives."

Blue seized upon the opportunity. "My home is here, young man. There seems to be some confusion. I'm living with my niece temporarily, and I'm happy with my situation."

That's when everyone looked at me. The cop did as well. They were expecting me to do something, Elie expecting me to back them up, Blue expecting me to defend her, and for one stunning moment, I couldn't think of one damn thing to say.

I stood there, horrified, at being placed in this position. And with everybody's eyes on me, I said, "She's my aunt and she doesn't want to go with them."

I looked back at Elie, disappointment in his eyes. Meredith was aghast. And so was Sally Ann. They left when the cop told them they couldn't take Blue against her will. That would be kidnapping. But before they left, I looked at Meredith and saw she had something sinister up her sleeve. She wasn't finished by a long shot, and the next time she came to visit, she fully intended to take Blue home.

~

At the office, I couldn't concentrate. I was an editorial consultant for the LSU Department of Pediatrics, and in the middle of applying for grants. We were hosting a medical symposium in December, and it was a busy time for me. I had to contact the guest speakers and arrange their travel and hotel accommodation. There were banquets during and following the symposium, and I had to organize them. There were a million other things to do. But my mind kept racing back to the gloom on my cousins' faces, their bewilderment and disappointment, when Blue refused to go home with them. I sat at my desk, guilt-ridden, as if I'd somehow abandoned Blue.

I had no idea what I was expecting myself to do, but I knew she needed me and that in some awful way I'd failed. I suspected my cousins felt the same, as if Blue had fallen down some mine shaft and we were powerless to help. I don't believe any of us were ready to say with certainty that Blue had turned senile, only that at some point, when our backs were turned, our dear Blue had walked away, never again to be seen alive. To a stranger, it might seem odd that the ordinary act of buying a building to start up a business would evoke such emotion in us. It's just that this wasn't Blue. I knew it. They knew it.

I sensed Blue knew it too, for if she were really telling me the truth and there wasn't some mental defect at play in all of this, if she really believed the Virgin Mary was calling on her for a purpose, felt something was being asked of her, she must be scared nearly out of her golfing clothes to come to a strange city and use up all her money (she'd inherited twice, I assumed, once from Uncle Imad and again from the Kaddoura family), to start a business or whatever you want to call it on the mystical orders of the Mother of Christ.

And how crazy was that?

Even to her.

The very thought of putting in plumbing and electricity and wiring and knocking down walls and dealing with the demands of the Louisiana Landmarks folks (she'd told me that old building had been nominated as a landmark), and complying with fire code regulations and requirements for the handicapped and bankers and loan officers and the bureaucratic demands for cooking in a commercial kitchen and getting a mixed-occupancy permit and liquor license and getting strangers to come together—*for what, I wanted to know?*—and trying to make ends meet with something that would never work, never in a million years, not to mention living on a street that was like a wilderness at night, would scare me into paralysis.

Blue had no idea what she was getting into.

All sorts of questions swirled inside my head.

~

*W*e were in my living room after supper, she on the sofa, I in the armchair. This time, I'd fixed the Screwdrivers. Blue sat in the middle of the sofa, wearing a turquoise skirt and a mint-green blouse. I don't ever recall seeing her in pants. She'd slipped off her shoes and was giving me the blow-by-blow on what happened after I left.

I'd gone back to the office, leaving Blue in the building. Sally Ann had called her on her cell, saying she would come back in a day or two, she and Meredith, to take her out to lunch. But Blue knew what that meant: She was going to drag her ass home.

She'd tried talking Sally Ann out of it, but Sally Ann refused to listen. And so Blue told me stoically she wasn't going to let that get her down. She felt thrilled—"Blessed," she called it—to be away from all the *hyazimme* our well-meaning family put her through, and would savor every moment of freedom for as long as it would last. (*Hyazimme* was an Arabic word, meaning chaos and confusion.) And she would raise her head above the turmoil. She had more important things to think about, like knocking down the front-room center wall.

"Why did you pick a building on Oretha Castle Haley?" I asked.

"Honey, I didn't pick it. I guess you could say it picked

45

me. I knew from the moment I saw it that I was destined to buy that building."

"Don't you think it may not be... *appropriate*? Good grief, Blue, if I were Lebanese, which, of course, you know I am, and looking for other Lebanese to socialize with, I might think twice before getting out of my car on that particular street. It's spooky, don't you think? Creepy. There's hardly anyone around, except homeless folks and drifters. It's Central City—high crime."

She didn't answer.

"I might go to the Lakefront," I babbled on. "Or Uptown. The Garden District. But Central City? Hell, no. You have to constantly be looking over your shoulder, worried some-one'll blow your head off."

She reached for some peanuts, popped them in her mouth. "Darlin'," she said, chewing. "I don't want you to misunderstand. I love Oretha Castle. I see its possibilities. But I recognize what others see: down-and-outers loitering around a homeless center, sleeping under an overpass. Winos roaming the streets, drinking from paper bags. Decent folks may not want to come. I'm fully aware of that."

"*Then why?*"

"I never would have chosen that street. Do you think I have no sense?"

She reached for more peanuts. They sat idle in her hand. "The very fact I'd never have chosen it but did, indeed, choose it because every cell in my body screamed at me to do it, tells me one thing: It was *Her* choice. Does that sound crazy?"

"'Her' meaning Mother Mary?"

She nodded.

"To some people, it might."

She leaned back, resting her head. The strain showed in

her face, worry lines around the eyes. Wearily, she stood up. "I guess I'll go refresh my drink."

"No, no, stay here." I took her glass to the kitchen and returned with a full pitcher. I placed her filled glass on the table. She acted as though she didn't see me, sunk in her jejune thoughts. I refilled my own drink, set the pitcher close to her. The noise must have startled her. She jolted.

"Jamila, you must be so confused."

"Well, yeah... *hello*! But there's another thing I want to know. Why Lebanese? Why's that in the plan, Blue?"

Blue brought the glass to her lips. She took a lingering sip and set it down. Imploringly, she looked at me. "Should I invite *abeid*?" she pondered. *"Yahoud?* Hispanics? Vietnamese? Should I invite anyone who wants to come, a mixture of everybody? Who should I invite? You see, I had no direction. I prayed to Mary to let me know Her purpose. I was hoping She'd pave the way so I wouldn't be so up in the air about everything. But apparently, this is to be a mystery. She doesn't want me to know too much. I've concluded She's trusting me to make the right choices, stay on the right path. And that She's guiding me every step of the way, because *how else am I to know?"*

For a moment, terror filled her eyes.

"And so," she continued forcefully, the fear inexplicably vanishing, "how will I know I'm doing Her will? The fact that I'm making these decisions under Her guidance. I have to *believe* She's with me through it all. I don't think She means to torture me. I think She means me to have a happy life."

Her eyes grew wide, startlingly blue.

"Sure," I said uncertainly. "But why *Lebanese?*"

She propped her feet on the coffee table. "My best thinking was Lebanese because that's all I know. I've hosted so many family parties. It was the first thing that came to mind. They're my *family*, Jamila. And that's a certain comfort.

And I've spent my whole life cooking Lebanese food. So why let that go to waste? But if this isn't Her will for me, I have to believe She'll find a way of telling me."

"Why didn't you tell Meredith and Sally Ann about the voice?"

"Honey, do you think they'd *believe* me? They'd think I was *majdoob*."

Majdoob meant a stupid person.

She reached for a clean napkin, folded it under her glass. "And then everything would go to pot. I'd be treated like a *majdoob*. Worse, as though dementia had set in. And when people tend to have a certain judgment of you, you begin to see yourself that way. If I've learned anything over the past eighty-one years, it's that if you truly believe in something, and only the deepest introspection can tell you if it's genuine, you have to stay the course. You *can't* give up. I have no intention of giving up. The simple fact is, Mary gave me a task. I don't know why. Or for what purpose. But if people want to think I'm crazy, there's nothing I can do about it. I know She'll always be with me. And that's enough to keep me going."

She searched my eyes for some belief.

"Do you remember telling me," I reminded her, "about how you sat in Fayad's hospital room all the time he was sick?"

She nodded.

"And that to keep yourself from losing it, you thought about all the good times—the family parties—over the years? And then you began fantasizing about the parties you'd give in the future? And how did these fantasies begin to occupy a special place in your heart? Do you remember telling me?"

"Yes."

"Blue, those fantasies were a way of coping, so you wouldn't be so upset about everything. It's hard losing people. And it's good to make plans. Do you think maybe the voice telling you to gather people together might be your way of dealing with all the deaths? That these fantasies were so real you confused them with divine purpose?"

I hurried on before she could stop me. "I read a book about Mother Teresa. It was a bunch of letters she wrote to a priest who was her spiritual advisor."

Head bowed, she looked up. "Yes, yes, I know that book."

"Well then, you must know that in her letters she writes about a mystical encounter with Christ. She said she heard the voice of Jesus, not once but repeatedly, over a period of months. Jesus spoke to her directly, and she knew it was Him speaking. She kept talking about the 'voice.' It was Him pleading with her directly to go carry His love to the 'poorest of the poor'—to the sick and dying and destitute in the worst slums of India. Well, this priest was skeptical. Mother Teresa wanted to start a new order of nuns, the Missionary Sisters of Charity. And the priest was afraid this was just a personal need and not a divine mission. And so he put her off for months. Then when he was sure this wasn't a personal crusade—a delusion—to fulfill her own private needs, but truly the will of Christ, he gave her permission to start the order and live in poverty and do this thing for the poor—"

"Yes, yes—"

"But, Blue," I cut her off, "this is the thing. I believe two things. I believe she really did hear the voice of Jesus. I have no doubt Mother Teresa heard it. But in reading all her letters, I had this feeling that all her life she had such a desperate need to help the poor that maybe, just maybe, the voice of Jesus and her own true passion combined together to become one. Do you see what I am saying? They were *not* two different things."

She thought about it and replied, "I see what you're saying." She started to say more, then stopped. She took a deep breath and let it out. "There's only one thing I know. *I wanted to go home.* I wanted to wake up on the Mississippi Coast in the worst way after my brother died. I wanted to see my old friends. Go to my Bible study. Be with my rosary group. Baby-sit my precious grandchildren. I missed my church." Tears welled in her eyes. She looked up, and a tired smile crept slowly across her face. "Honey, do you think in a million years I'd be doing this if I didn't have to?"

The glow of lamplight cast a shadow across the sofa. Behind it, between the parted curtains, holly leaves pressed against the darkened window, stirring in the moonless sky.

"Well, Blue," I said reluctantly. I shook my head, threw up my arms, and gave off a heavy sigh. "I give up. I surrender. Let's get this crazy show on the road."

CHAPTER 5

$\mathcal{I}$n the succeeding days, Blue worked in the grueling heat alongside Alejandro, Evandro, and Otavio. Money seemed to be a worry for her; she wasn't sure if she could get a loan. I never asked about her personal wealth or how much she had inherited, figuring that was none of my business.

She knew the renovations would cost at least several hundred thousand, and so to save on expenses, she decided against leasing or buying a car, at least for the time being. I began dropping her off at the building each morning and, if she needed to go somewhere later, Alejandro would give her a ride.

I'd pick her up after work, leaving my office a little after five, unless the doctors needed me to stay late, and wait outside with the motor running. We'd have supper at some café or fix a simple meal at home. And she'd fill me in on the day's activities. Alejandro and the Brazilians usually worked 'til the light faded before heading back to their place: Alejandro's one-room apartment on Palmyra Street in Mid-City.

From what I could tell, Alejandro was the only one of the three of them here in this country legally.

Alejandro was in charge when it came to the work, putting into action Blue's grand schemes and plans. And if I were a religious woman (though I could never be as devout as her), I'd swear God dropped him from the sky to be a guardian angel to her. She was curious when it came to her three guys. And, sometimes, when I'd hang out on weekends, I'd watch how the Mississippi Delta belle operated when it came to learning about their lives. She'd be busy doing something, sweeping, dusting the banisters, when out of nowhere and with great delicacy, some personal question would ooze out of her honey mouth.

We learned that Alejandro was born in Mexico City, the eldest of eleven kids. His parents owned a modest home, and his papa drove a cab. He'd attended college on an art scholarship and painted on the streets of San Antonio before heading for the Big Easy immediately following the storm. He went about his duties quietly, occasionally taking road trips to Mexico to purchase ornate doors and windows, magnificently beautiful, in my opinion, at outrageously low prices.

And Blue loved what he brought back, loved what her building would become, as though she'd stumbled upon the magic of transforming something old into a work of art. As for Alejandro, he craved going back to Mexico as often as he could to get items for the building. He was homesick for his country and had a son living there. He didn't speak as freely as the Brazilians, only answering whatever Blue would ask, and only once did he mention a son. Blue was discreet and knew better than to pry. But I often wondered about his silence, whether it was from the sadness of their separation or some shame he wouldn't identify. The one thing he did say was that his dream was to one day return to Mexico to start his own business, an art gallery or café, so that he'd have a legacy to leave his son.

And they were a great team.

Evandro and Otavio were kind, communicating their respect for her in ways beyond language. But as much as Blue adored them, she pitied them even more. They couldn't afford to bring their families here. Alejandro said they wanted to relocate their families (since New Orleans reminded them of São Paulo) and would do so once they found steady work. It was only a matter of time. Evandro's wife lived in Connecticut with their three sons, and Otavio's family was in Atlanta, with a son and a daughter. Blue sensed their loneliness. They often showed her photos of their kids and beamed over the fuss she made. On Sundays, they went to a Portuguese-language Mass at St. Anthony of Padua, and, of course, that thrilled Blue.

And so the days passed harmoniously.

'Til one day I noticed something odd.

Blue would often forget what she was about to say or couldn't think of a word she wanted to use. It was upsetting. Her memory had always been good. Or she'd stand in the center of the room, forgetting where she was, then a period of time would pass before, shrugging it off, she'd once again go about her duties. I couldn't get over the way she acted. She'd always been alert before. But I dismissed it, thinking it normal for a woman her age, and it didn't necessarily mean anything terrible was happening to her.

Until something happened to make me believe we had more pressing matters on our hands.

CHAPTER 6

*I*t was Friday. The light had faded. I had arrived a little late. I'd decided to get out of my car and go into the building to take a look at the week's work.

Inside, it was sweltering hot, and everything was a mess. The interior wall was being knocked down, as was a second staircase, to make more space for the kitchen. Evandro and Otavio greeted me and returned to what they were doing, oblivious to the racket of banging hammers and falling wood as Blue and I made our way upstairs. She was eager to show me what Alejandro had brought back from Mexico, all items salvaged from demolished buildings: a battered mesquite interior door, an iron chandelier with ribbed alabaster glass shades, and terra cotta tiles. I was admiring all these beautiful things in the waning light from the gallery window—the fine craftsmanship, cheap prices—when we heard shouting from the floor below.

Alejandro bolted. Blue and I scrambled downstairs. Scuffling noises could be heard coming from the front entrance. As we got closer, we saw Evandro and Otavio in a tangle with two men. The rapacious eyes of one of the intruders completely captured my attention as he grabbed a toolbox from his friend. A toothpick dangled from his mouth, and his face was lean. He was dressed all in black—black tee, jeans. A cap covered his head and, when Evandro managed to knock it off, exposed a bald, caramel-colored skull. He had thick brows and an expression that never lost its intensity as, moments after grabbing the toolbox, he leaped down the porch steps with the toolbox under one arm.

Evandro and Otavio weren't about to let his comrade go.

They grabbed him, pulling him down. And that's when Alejandro came running. Seeing Alejandro, Otavio released his hold on the stranger and took off at full speed with nothing on his mind but getting his toolbox back. Now the stranger and Evandro were battling it out, Evandro struggling on the floor to get on top of him, sweat dripping from him, and in a move too swift to see, a blade ascending. Alejandro, several feet away, might as well have been in Mexico. The knife stuck out of Evandro's upper arm and, as Evandro looked down, he jerked back, gritting teeth, and that was when the intruder scrambled to his feet and flew out the door like a bird with a cat behind him.

Blue screamed. Alejandro was on his knees, carefully guiding the knife out of Evandro's arm. He took off his shirt, stripped it, and bound a strip around the bleeding wound.

"Get him to the car," Blue wailed. "We'll take him to Touro—"

Blood gushed from Evandro. Blue, on her knees, enfolded him, the pupils of her eyes darting from Evandro to Alejandro to me. Alejandro whispered to Evandro, and Evandro shook his head.

"He will not go," Alejandro interpreted.

"He has to," Blue pleaded, her summer dress drenched in red-vermilion. "He'll bleed to death. Can't you reason with him?"

"He thinks he will be deported."

I looked out the door, trying to catch a glimpse of Otavio, as the entire recumbent Boulevard lapsed into darkness; eerie and sepulchral, shadowy buildings to my right and left. And then it came to me: Dr. U.

Dr. U was an emergency-room pediatrician.

A native of Peru, he'd worked at University Hospital for all the time I'd known him. His name was Carlos Angelito Ugarteche, but everyone called him Dr. U. Standing in the pediatric emergency room on the rare days we weren't busy, he would regale us with stories about Arequipa, where the grateful parents of all the children he tended would pay him with little gifts: live chickens, sacks of potatoes. And when the hospital flooded after Katrina and the Pediatric Emergency Room was shut down, our Department was moved to Children's Hospital, which was quite all right with me. It was Uptown, near my home, an easy commute, and I liked it. I also liked Dr. U. I knew he wasn't working a shift that night because I'd prepared the attendants' schedule myself.

"Dr. U will help," I blurted out. "We'll go to his house. He'll take good care of Evandro. He won't report him!" I reached for my cell, but Evandro snatched it away from me.

"No get excited... no panic...," Alejandro reassured Evandro, relieving him of the phone and giving it back to me.

"I know what we'll do," I said, putting the phone away. "I have a first-aid kit at home. We'll go there. I have bandages under the bathroom sink."

Standing in the doorway, Otavio rushed to Evandro, nearly slipping in the pool of blood. And when I glanced back at the entrance, I couldn't believe what I was seeing. Standing in the spot where Otavio had been moments before were Meredith and Sally Ann.

*T*he first-aid kit was one I'd bought for one of our region's many storms. Inside were cleaning wipes, band-aids, Tylenol, surgical dressings, and step-by-step directions for any type of emergency. In bold letters, the instructions read: "DO NOT remove a protruding object." But it was way too late for that.

In the bathroom of my home, Alejandro lowered the lid of the toilet seat. He removed the tourniquet from Evandro and motioned him to sit. Evandro had sustained a deep wound, to the bone, and blood gushed from his arm onto the pink tiles and turquoise mat. We moved him to the side of the tub. Alejandro splashed peroxide over the wound and took out a needle and thread from a silver box I'd handed him (a long-ago gift from Aunt Marcia) and threaded it. He took out a cigarette lighter, sterilized the needle, and began suturing the wound himself.

Blue's idea of an anesthetic was a bottle of champagne I'd been saving. Sitting next to Evandro, she made sure he drank it and, what little was left, she drank herself. I worked for doctors but couldn't stand anything sticking in the skin, and so I got myself a beer, settled in the living room, and waited for it to be over. Meredith and Sally Ann sat stiffly on the couch, and it was plain from Meredith's face that the best part of her day was when she wagged her finger, smiled wickedly at Blue, and said, "You see! I *told* you so..." After Evandro had been bandaged and lay resting in the guest room, his clothes tumbling in the washer, Blue and I took our separate baths and changed our bloody clothes.

~

"*I told you*," Meredith shrieked. "*Told you*, but you wouldn't listen. Remember when I *told* you somebody was gonna get *killed*?"

"Nobody got killed," I fumed. "Do you have to be so dramatic?"

We were seated at the dining table, eating baloney and cheese sandwiches. Blue scooped up a cherry from the store-bought pink lemonade.

"Listen, Blue," Meredith lectured. "This could have been *you*. Sure as I'm sitting here, these animals will be back tomorrow to get whatever else they want."

"Oh, for Christ's sake," I groaned, "don't get your nose so out of joint!"

"And you..."—Sally Ann said, shaking her finger—"all you ever do is goad her on!"

"I had *nothing* to do with this—"

"Stop bickering!" said Blue. "There's something I want to tell you."

Meredith got up, began pacing.

"Will you please sit down," Blue bristled, "and listen to me for once?"

Meredith sat down.

"Give me two weeks to pack and conclude my business here, and I will come back with you to Harbortown. The only thing I ask..."—and here Blue turned to Sally Ann—"is that you have enough decency and respect to let me leave with my pride and dignity."

We sat back, pondering this.

"Do you promise?" Sally Ann said presently.

"I do." Blue nodded.

Blue had always been truthful, never making promises she couldn't keep, and so Sally Ann began to relax. "Okay," said Sally Ann, "but I want to make one thing clear: in two weeks, we will be back. And don't you *dare* try anything sneaky 'cause Frankie and Elie will be coming too."

Blue didn't miss a beat.

"And now that's settled,"—she tossed back her head—"do you gals want to stay the night? You can leave tomorrow morning. I'll fix shrimp and grits for breakfast."

Sally Ann said no, Frankie was expecting her that night. She took her plate to the kitchen, with Meredith trotting behind. After they'd finished washing dishes, Blue saw them to their car. She asked them not to tell Frankie and Elie about the *hyazimme* back at the building, then waved 'til they were out of sight. She returned, sat where she was sitting before. Her face resting in her hands, she slowly lifted herself up and, with relief shining in her eyes, said to no one in particular, "Darlin', let's get a dog."

"What?"

"A puppy." Blue responded, popping another cherry in her mouth. "We'll teach him to be a watchdog. We'll go tomorrow to Animal Rescue. And we'll get an alarm system for extra protection."

"No," Alejandro insisted, reaching past me for a pickle. "No want alarm... Not when we must work..."

"Hey, I hate to interrupt you two," I said, "but what about Meredith and Sally Ann?"

"We'll turn it on at night." Blue's eyes fixed on Alejandro.

"And we no want dog," Alejandro said adamantly. "We no be watching dog. Dog big trouble."

"Hey," I raised my voice, "what about Meredith and Sally Ann?"

"We'll put him in the back yard for now,"—Blue would not be interrupted—"and build a doghouse to protect him. Later, we'll build a fence 'round the property so he can roam free wherever he likes. And we'll put lights outside as well."

~

*I*n the days that followed, Blue wouldn't let Evandro do any work, though she paid him anyway. And the next day she got a pup—a female mutt, part Belgian Malinois. It was playful, spirited, and looked mean but wasn't. Alejandro named her Pelusa— "mischievous one" or "street kid" in Spanish—and Blue delighted in that. But the purchase of a security system had to wait. Blue was bleeding money. The banks had turned her down for a loan.

It was no surprise.

It was 2009, when the country was going through one of its worst economic downturns, and banks weren't lending money, especially to octogenarians who wouldn't live long enough to pay them back. She even applied for government grants through the Redevelopment Authority, but that, too, went belly up. And so Blue was reduced to making every purchase out of pocket. Seeing the work ahead, I estimated the renovations would cost at least four hundred thousand. But Blue was determined the café would survive and even thrive. She even boasted it'd make a profit in its first year, her unwavering optimism completely lost on me.

More and more, I was beginning to worry. The things she said and things she did didn't make any sense to me. She wasn't the practical person I'd known in Harbortown.

And she never used to break promises. But on the day my cousins arrived, she borrowed Alejandro's old jeep and high-tailed it to Pontchatoula, Louisiana, on the pathetic excuse of visiting a sick friend, leaving me the noxious task of explaining to them where she was.

That bothered me.

As did a lot of other things.

Against all rationality, she was throwing away her inheritance with no possibility of getting it back. I assumed the cost of renovating the building was coming entirely from her personal wealth. Uncle Imad had been a wealthy business-man, having succeeded as a merchant and developer his entire life. I wasn't worried she'd starve to death when this adventure of hers failed; still, it seemed a waste of money, though I never said a word to her. More and more, I felt sad for her since big troubles seemed all but inevitable.

One night, I dreamed Blue and I were passengers on a rogue streetcar racing toward a crossing truck while the conductor sat in the driver's seat with foam oozing from his mouth, spilling out like an overflowing tub in rivulets of blood on the floor as we waited, panic-stricken, bracing for the accident.

And, sure enough, big trouble did come to her sooner than I expected.

CHAPTER 7

$\mathcal{S}$ ince six-month-old Pelusa was wildly playful, the men insisted she stay in the back yard, at least 'til she got older. Evandro and Otavio decided to sleep upstairs at night to keep an eye on the place, and sometimes they'd take turns sleeping on the gallery where they could catch a warm breeze.

If Blue didn't break a sweat over the future of her café, she worried ceaselessly about her "boys." She didn't want them sleeping in the building. It wasn't safe, she told them.

But speaking through Alejandro, who interpreted for them, they convinced her they'd be fine, saying it'd only be a matter of months before the work would be completely finished and she could finally move in. By that time, the alarm system would be installed and the fence erected, with Pelusa roaming the grounds to scare off marauding visitors.

It was inconceivable to me that Blue would live in that place.

But that had always been her plan.

And so as the days moved on and Blue's "boys" concentrated on their work, I began noticing things about Blue. At my house one night, she insisted on baking meat pies, a favorite Lebanese staple she could make blindfolded with her hands tied. But when I bit into my meat pie, I couldn't believe what I was eating. She'd forgotten to add the ground beef. That same night, she dumped a bowl of peanuts in the sink with the dirty dishes. Another night, we were gossiping about Meredith and Sally Ann, as we loved to do after supper, and she couldn't remember their names. This was appalling to me. That night, I got down on my knees and prayed for my sweet Blue.

Next morning, when I awoke, I found her toothpaste tube and toothbrush in the fridge on top of the Saran-wrapped Pyrex pan containing the left-over eggplant casserole. Three days later, she reached into her purse to pay Alejandro in cash and, instead of pulling out two grand, proceeded to add another. Alejandro corrected her and gave her back her money, but my knees began to shake thinking of the implications of what that meant.

I wasn't sure what I should do.

And when one isn't sure, one usually does nothing, which is exactly what I did. And so life continued on. In the weeks that followed, as I became increasingly busy with my work, she was in a tizzy to get the building finished so she could host her grand opening party. It was her most fervent desire, her most passionate wish. I wondered—once the party was over—whether she thought her duty to Mary would be over too. That the business would run itself and she could hightail it back to Harbortown? I honestly didn't know what she thought. Was she counting on Mary to tell her what to do? Because if that was her thinking, she'd be waiting a long time.

But this wasn't my problem. I was only here to help. I didn't run the whole shebang. Wasn't in charge of squat. You can't force people to act rationally, can't force them to face reality. And I was not going to let this get to me. But looking back on it, I was worried. And as the days meandered on, I knew I had plenty of reason.

~

*I*t happened on a Saturday, in late October. I'd put in a couple of hours overtime at the hospital, then came back in the afternoon to hang out at the building when I saw Alejandro standing on the sidewalk, gazing at the backs of three teens passing on our block. I was watering the dwarf yaupons some young Evangelical Lutheran volunteers had planted when Blue approached Alejandro.

"Honey, I've been thinking..." She stood cheerfully before him. "It looks like the renovations will be finished by December. So I thought we'd do our party on...," Blue looked befuddled, "... on... on..." Her eyes moved in her head, chasing her elusive thoughts. "on... Thursday... December 10th. The opening—on my birthday. I'll be 82, you know."

When Alejandro didn't answer, she followed his gaze to some young men passing by the Jacob Lawrence Gallery. One, a gangling youth well over six feet, three, looking like a giant between two midgets, wore loose jeans and Gucci loafers. One of the shorter youths wore a brown shirt with eagle wings. As they wandered up the street, Alejandro couldn't take his eyes off them.

"Is there something wrong?" Blue asked.

"I'm sorry. What did you say?"

"You look concerned. Did something happen?"

"I no worry," Alejandro said, frowning. "It's just that... every time I say hello they no say hello back. They give me dirty look."

"Who?"

"The Blacks who pass by."

"What kind of dirty look?"

"I do not know how to explain."

"They always say hello to me."

"You see," Alejandro said gruffly, "this is the thing: Evandro and Otavio will practice their English on them, say 'good morning,' 'good afternoon,' and they walk by, no say a word. No smile, nothing. But you and Jamila—they greet you like queens. No like us, no respect."

"'Us' meaning Latinos?" I'd been sitting on the porch steps, uncapping a water bottle after putting away the garden hose. I walked over and joined them.

"Yes," Alejandro muttered, gazing forlornly at the street. "They think Latino bad word. Does not make sense. There is this... I do not know... is not like this in San Antonio."

"That's because San Antonio's mostly Latino. Things are different here."

"Yes, yes. *Racista.*"

Blue looked in the direction of the boys, now diminishing figures in the distance. "Maybe they think Latinos have come to take their jobs, honey. So many moved here after the storm, looking for work. It might be a territorial thing."

Silently, I agreed. There'd been rumblings of discontent between the races. It was common knowledge that Latinos were labeled "walking ATM machines." Many were undocumented workers who, unable to open bank accounts, kept their wages in their pockets and were easy targets for robberies.

But the robberies couldn't be blamed on any one race. Latinos were abused by everybody. They were particularly abused by White contractors who promised to pay them to repair a house, then left them hanging after the work was done. It had happened so many times that the city council was working on passage of an ordinance to allow the handcuffing and booking of anyone who committed "wage theft," considered a particular form of robbery. But this was not what Alejandro was talking about. He was talking about the Blacks who wandered past our building.

"I have bad feeling," he murmured.

"What kind of bad feeling?"

"Do not know how to explain it. This is mostly Black street. They do not like us and it's no good."

"Try being positive," Blue replied gently. "It's important to get along."

~

On Sunday, I was finishing watering the bushes. I'd unscrewed the garden hose and arranged it in a circle. After picking up Pelusa's water bowl, I stood over the faucet to refill it. Near the street, a teenager was dumping trash into one of our garbage cans.

"My friend," Alejandro called out. He was sitting on the front porch, stretching out his legs, holding onto a can of beer. "My friend... excuse me, my friend... I do not know if you know but these are our cans."

The boy—he was young—appeared not to be listening. And as he lifted the lid off another can, Alejandro called out a second time. "Son, you are welcome to use the cans today but no more. No more—we need them."

As the youth threw the trash bag into the can, he shouted back at Alejandro: "This don't belong to you." He nodded in the direction of the building. "Who the fuck you think you are?" Black stripes covered the upper portion of his over-sized shirt, the lower portion a flaming yellow. He wore a cap with a visor turned to face the back of his head. A black elastic net hugged his skull.

Alejandro put down his beer. He descended the steps and headed toward the boy. Momentarily, he stood before him.

"My name Alejandro Cruz." He reached out to offer his hand. "I work for the woman who own this building. My pleasure to meet you. And your name?"

The boy studied him. He had a pretty face, like a young Michael Jackson, but with ruthlessly questioning eyes. They were demanding eyes, impertinent, an attitude out of sync with his delicate nose and shapely lips.

Alejandro's hand remained extended. He wore a strained smile. The boy put back the lid. He turned to Alejandro and, with perfect clarity, said, "My name ain't none of yo business, dawg."

Alejandro withdrew his hand. "You do not have to talk to me that way," he said. "You are welcome to use our cans this time, but no more, my friend. We must finish our work."

"Nigga spic." The boy walked off.

He crossed the street, keeping a steady pace. There was a slight bounce to his step as he entered the Frederick Douglass Center. I'd been leaning over the faucet, about to turn on the water. I put down the bowl and walked over to where Alejandro stood.

"What the hell just happened?"

Alejandro didn't answer. He gazed steadily at the Center. Morosely, he turned and trudged silently to our building, looking like an overloaded dump truck had landed on his head. He disappeared inside. I turned and stared across the street, wondering what I'd do and say if I ever got the nerve to go over there and have a showdown with that boy.

CHAPTER 8

$\mathcal{I}$ entered the Frederick Douglass Center and proceeded ahead for seven feet or more before turning to face the entrance to an office on my left. The office door was open. Inside, the boy stood in front of a desk, looking down at a woman seated behind the desk.

The woman's skin was copper-toned, hair blonde with shiny highlights, wavy in a professional cut, the shape and texture of a wig, only I didn't think it was a wig. She was heavy-set, the upper arms thick as a muscle-builder's, only flaccid. She wore a diaphanous black short-sleeved blouse with a lacy white under-blouse. Large silver bracelets dangled from her wrist.

She glanced my way before turning to the boy and saying something, and he turned to look at me. He didn't appear to recognize me, and I suspected he hadn't seen me during his exchange with Alejandro.

"Can I help?" the woman asked.

"My name's Jamila," I said, stepping in. "I was wondering if I might have a word with this young man. After you get through, of course."

She came to me and offered her hand, saying, "I'm Odessa Morgan. And you?"

Her eyes were large, luminous, and dark, her brows light and high above the eyes. It may have been the combination of fleshy roundness, soft radiance of skin and sensitivity of expression that gave off such a youthful glow. Still, I had the feeling she was at least my age.

"I'm the director here," she added.

"Pleased to meet you, Ms. Morgan." I reached out to shake her hand. "The lady who owns the building across the street —you might know her—Blue. I'm her niece."

"Yes, yes—Blueberry." She smiled. "She came over to introduce herself. I asked about her name, and she gave me the full-blown treatment. Said her full name...

... let me see if I can recall... wait, I wrote it down..." She went to her desk, glanced at some scribbling on a small notepad, and said, "...Bahia Bechara Kaddoura Hamieh. Yes, that's what she told me. We had quite a laugh about that. We're happy to have her in the 'hood. Call me Odessa, everybody does."

She waited for me to state my business. I had a momentary lapse of courage, wanting to make some excuse and walk away, or maybe continue with the polite chitchat, only I was fresh out of chitchat, so I decided to speak plainly.

"I'd like to talk to him about what happened a few minutes ago," I blurted out. "I think I might have misunderstood. I was hoping he'd clear things up."

She turned. "This is Lennus Butler, my assistant Alice's child. He helps out when we need him."

He threw off that inquisitive look, like he was demanding to know what I wanted. It was almost vicious in its insistence, blunted once more by the delicacy of his physical beauty.

"I think you should know," she lowered her voice, "he was telling me what happened. I'm glad you came over."

"What did he say?"

"Please sit down, dear," she said to Lennus. She motioned me to a chair next to him. And there we sat, the boy and I, in front of Odessa's desk, and it was like I was way back in grammar school, in the principal's office waiting to be punished.

"Lennus," Odessa said encouragingly, "why don't you tell her what you told me."

He was slumped in his chair, biding his time. "Ain't nothing to tell," he said, drumming his fingers on the armrest. "I put my bags in the cans and this dude, he say, 'Get outta here, nigga'."

He folded his hands over his nose, forming a perfect triangle before rubbing his tattooed arm. He couldn't have been more than a hundred and twenty pounds and five-feet-seven or so. The tattoos started at his wrist, moving up the arm, disappearing under the sleeve, looking like the busy pattern of a long-sleeved shirt.

Odessa nodded. "Go on."

"I tell him I'm sorry. He say he gone slit my throat. I say, 'Hold your horses, dude. I ain't here to cause no trouble.' He raise his fist to hit me—"

"Wait a minute...," I interrupted. "Alejandro's who he's talking about. He works for my aunt. He would never say or do anything like that. I was there. He's making it up."

It was impossible to read her face. I started to get up; she motioned me to remain seated.

"Is this true?" She nodded to the boy.

He slumped deeper in his chair, legs apart, looking placid, in no hurry. He lowered his chin, but his eyes met hers. "You ask anybody who pass by that joint that dude rant at everybody: He gone get his gun and shoot us. That's what he tell us. You ask anybody—they know."

"What were you doing putting trash in their cans?"

"Didn't know it was theirs."

"It was across the street?"

"Yep."

"In front of their building?"

"Uh-huh."

"Well, then," Odessa's voice took on a sterner note, "*whose* did you think they were? They certainly weren't ours. Next time, put our trash in *our* cans. You know where they are."

"That don't give him no right to raise his fist—"

"*Odessa... Ms. Morgan*," I protested, "Alejandro's not that way. He's a gentleman. He's decent. I don't understand why he's saying these things."

Her face remained impassive. "Bring him over. We'll straighten it out." And then she turned to look at the boy. "You stay here. She'll go get him."

I crossed the street, all the time thinking about Lennus. He couldn't have been more than fifteen. Yet, at no time in our brief acquaintance did his eyes give the slightest hint he was a lying little jerk. Hard-core, street punk.

I brought Alejandro over, hauling Blue along with him. Odessa and Lennus looked up as we came in. A warm smile appeared on Odessa's lips at the first sighting of my aunt. But when Blue settled in her chair, Odessa slipped back into her former self: the consummate professional mediator. She brought in some folding chairs, told us Lennus's mom was sick. Otherwise, she'd be joining us. The room felt cramped. I was getting claustrophobic as she shut the door, deciding to concentrate on a pale-blue vase of yellow roses.

Odessa sat back, explained the reason for our visit. Eyes on Alejandro, she said, "Who wants to go first?"

"I do not have anything against this boy," Alejandro said

71

with feeling. "But the thing he say no good. I want him to say he sorry."

At Odessa's urging, Alejandro told his side of the story. Afterwards, Odessa turned to the boy. "We have two completely different versions here, Lennus. Are you sure you heard what you heard?" She waited two heartbeats. "Now, be careful, Lennus. It seems to me that if a man threatens to slit throats and beat up people and shoot them we've got a raving lunatic on our hands. Your allegations are quite serious. Are you sure you're telling the truth?"

Lennus looked her in the eye and said through gritted teeth: "You tell this asshole go back where he come from."

"Mexico?" Alejandro said heatedly. "Is that where you want me to go?"

"I don't give a shit—Mexico, Cuba, Guatemala, Colombia, Nicaragua, Brazil—you go where you go. You don't belong here. Nobody want you—"

"What did we do to you? Why do you hate us?"

"Don't hate you, dawg. Don't give a fuck 'bout you."

"I don't believe you." Alejandro was three seats from the boy. He leaned his elbows against his knees, looking sideways at him. "I don't believe anyone who say the things you say can be anything but a hater. I do not leave here 'til you tell me why you call me 'spic.'"

With the slur meeting daylight, Blue turned her head and shuddered. She was seated to the right of Alejandro, next to the boy. She lowered her head, arched it to the side, leaning toward Lennus and away from us. Odessa showed no emotion. She conducted herself with remarkable grace, I thought, reminding me of a counselor who's pretty much heard everything, far worse than in this room. The silence lingered. Alejandro wouldn't budge.

It seemed to get to the boy.

"I call you that," he said, flashing his contempt, "'cause you got no right being here. They's folks lived here all they life been away four years and you ain't got no right taking they place."

"What on earth are you talking about?" Blue wanted to know.

"Talking 'bout *him.*"

The boy's eyes frightened me. He and Blue were inches apart, staring at each other.

"Most my friends, they never come back. There's no place for 'em. Anything lef' cost too much. 'Cause of *you.*" He glared at Alejandro. "You and yours. Fourteen thousand spic move here after the storm, now there's tens of thousands more—completely taking over."

"Listen," Odessa scolded, "you can't use that language in this room. This man's not to blame for what happened to our people. He helped us. He *rebuilt.* This city wouldn't have moved forward if it hadn't been for his people. You should be grateful, Lennus."

"Grateful? For taking our jobs, our cribs? Ain't enough jobs 'fore the storm. Hardly any lef'—"

"We take *nobody's* jobs," Alejandro erupted. "We take the jobs nobody *want.* We sweat all the time in the heat and filth, gutting houses, cleaning debris, building roofs, working seven days a week, doing dangerous work. We break our backs rebuilding, repairing your ruined homes. We sleep on floor. Ten to room. In the country. Tents. You think we can afford the rents either?"

"You take our jobs, motherfucka—"

"Stop it," Odessa demanded. *"You stop it right now!"*

"Go home, fucka." The boy's eyes were daggers. "Ain't no rebuilding lef'. It's time you go home!" He leaped from his chair and lunged for the door, slamming it behind him but not before getting in one last dig: "Either you go home, or I swear to God we coming after you..."

It was as if they'd been alone, Alejandro and Lennus, the heat of their outrage extinguishing the rest of us. We couldn't find our voices. A malaise had settled in, an ugly, disheartening quiet. Blue, deeply affected, stepped behind the desk to hug Odessa before leaving the room. I could see her shoulders tremble. Alejandro and I soon followed. We walked back to the building, dazed and shaken, before a deep sadness dug in. We started on our chores, anything to keep busy, Alejandro laying tile, Blue bathing Pelusa, me scrubbing floors.

~

In the kitchen, I was on my hands and knees when the memories came floating down, enveloping me like a heavy fog. It was Mardi Gras Day 2006, barely six months after the storm, when hundreds of thousands of Blacks still hadn't come home. I was trotting down St. Charles Avenue chasing after the floats, seeing the masses of White faces, hearing their laughter, but there wasn't a single Black person anywhere, and I felt strangely alone. There was an emptiness amid the celebration, a joylessness in the streets, if one paid attention, an ineffable spirit missing.

I remembered the long ride out. I was among hundreds of thousands on the interstate highway, heading west in the contra flow at three in the morning, one day before Katrina, enduring a normally seven-hour ride to Austin in an agonizing eighteen. I'd left my cats back home. I thought it best. They hated evacuations (we'd been through so many), the long hours in cages, the road sickness, the strange surroundings. And so I thought I was being merciful. I'd left plenty of food and water. And besides, it wouldn't be long. I'd be back in a day or two.

And like everybody else, I watched the catastrophe:

babies at the Convention Center in the oven-like heat; families in boats; children on roofs; the interview with the widower who'd let his wife's hand slip because he couldn't hold it any longer, sinking into the water; our mayor; police chief; Oprah with her handkerchief, dread in her eyes, stepping into the Superdome. On TV, I watched—mesmerized and horrified—with one bright shining hope: *I'll be home soon, home to my baby cats, and soon it'll be over.*

We heard about a breach. No big deal. An evacuee sitting next to me in the hotel lobby, where we had all gathered to watch the horror and avoid being alone, began praising the Army Corps. He believed in their competence, convinced that this group of expert engineers had long been on the scene, was way on top of things, doing whatever was needed to patch things up—or whatever one does when a levee breaches. I kept waiting for the news, like at a football game when you don't understand the sport and rely on the roar of the crowd to know who's winning. But here, the "voices" never lifted, dragging us down into an unfathomable circumstance.

We saw the waters rise.

I'm ashamed to say that in the midst of all this suffering, the only thing I could think about was my cats back home. Were they afraid? Desperate? Did they think I had abandoned them? It had never entered my mind, amidst the chaos and craziness, that my house might be underwater and, with it, my cats—the grace of God shielding me. The authorities demanded that we stay where we were. We weren't going anywhere. But at four in the morning in the first week of September I filled my can with gas, got on the dark highway, knowing that at some point I'd have to elude the National Guard, sneak on the back roads to dodge the barricades, give them some false story in case I got caught, and hope they wouldn't shoot me.

I made it to River Road and then to Magazine and then to Octavia and, in the best moment of my life, parked in front of my house. It was just as I'd left it. I live in the high part, the "sliver on the river," the twenty percent of the city that had escaped the flood. I ran to my guestroom, poked my head under the bed, grabbed my cats, hustled them into their carriers, and hauled them to the car. A Blackhawk helicopter hovered overhead, thinking I was a looter. I waved and smiled and absconded to Natchitoches, Louisiana, to crash with a dear friend. It was there I stayed 'til they said we could come home. But all of this is leading up to what I really want to tell you.

What I really want to tell you is how it feels when death comes. There was another couple in Natchitoches staying with my friend. I knew the man but didn't know his girl-friend. We watched TV together, all of us and our hostess, listening for any sign the city would survive, the girlfriend on alert to reinforce her gleeful wish that New Orleans would go under, destroyed forever, for reasons I don't understand.

She was thrilled when they said the pollution would kill us, the water supply was contaminated, too many chemicals in the air, it would never be safe again. And city services would stop because no taxes could be collected. With each dire prediction, the girlfriend perked up. She was planning her escape—anywhere but New Orleans—to Maine, Vermont. She had a fine time researching the demographics of each new home, awaiting her adventure. And when it was announced another storm was on its way, she said to her boyfriend, "Let's hope it hits New Orleans and spares Texas."

I learned a long time ago, years before Katrina, that this city was my best friend. This is the thing: when I arrived in September and drove up St. Charles, dodging the branches and fallen power lines, without a single soul around, no birds, squirrels, a hush blanketing the city in an eerie death watch, I saw an oak tree on the neutral ground with a home-made sign on it that read in bold letters, "Now you know what it means to miss New Orleans." And I knew I'd never leave this place.

I'd be the last crazy old lady hanging out at Harry's Bar, bumming around the streets with ducks waddling after her, waiting for death to come. And surely it would. And I knew what it would look like: Ruined houses. Flooded cars. Dead bodies in water. Drowned trees—thousands—victims of the stagnant water that lingered for weeks.

In the beginning, I only drove through the best parts of town, unable to face Lakeview, Gert Town, the Lower 9. But later, when I did, death fell like dust, burying me alive. And then one night, a friend came to get me out of the gloom of night to take me to Jackson Square to enter St. Louis Cathedral, where a Christmas concert was underway.

This is what I want to tell you: For the first time in my life, I celebrated something more than me. As we entered the Cathedral, we saw the backs of many people—gays, Blacks, children, old folks—crammed into pews and jammed into aisles, listening to the most beautiful operatic voices. And I wanted to scream in that vast space, thrust my arms high, scramble into pews, trample over feet, and squeeze these people. The next night, at a candle-lighting ceremony in Washington Square attended by a smaller gathering, smiles lit up the park as if we'd won the Super Bowl because we were all there together in our jeans and tennis shoes, holding candles, singing carols.

I am fifty-one years old. I have seen a lot of death. All I wanted was to live.

And this is what I want to say: It's all the same, really, the New Year's Eve parties at Blue's, the picnics on the beach with my mom and dad. Or Uncle Imad's barbeques. Or waking up Christmas morning to sneak down the stairs of my beautiful home with all my cousins from Alabama to find the presents Santa left. Or what happened years ago, if I can summon my imagination to picture the merchants along Oretha Castle Haley Boulevard gathered in the morning light to chatter and open shop and welcome their customers from Ireland and Italy and Russia and Germany, or the hundreds of Blacks not welcomed on Canal, all come to the Boulevard to celebrate the day in the company of others.

And how could they know, these ghosts of the Boulevard, that one day in the year 2009 a woman like me—a Mississippi girl—or a woman like Blue—an old-timer from the Delta—would gather once again to duplicate their efforts and honor them and plan for the many years to come with even more celebrations, because we are sick and tired of death.

And who will come?

~

I looked up from the floor to see Blue standing over me.

"I have an idea how we can straighten things out." Blue reached for my hand. "Let's go find Odessa."

In my head, I replayed the video of her New Year's Eve parties and saw Blue with black hair, dewy olive skin, a long nose, high cheekbones, and perfectly carved features. She looked like a beauty queen. And her disposition was happy. She wasn't sweet or delicate, domineering or overpowering, holy or self-righteous, but a lovely, joyous woman whose actions through the years reflected kindness—humility—that was neither conspicuous nor self-serving.

On this day, as she looked down, I saw the same woman, really, only whose hips had widened, who had crows-feet and sagging jowls and liver spots and hair dyed auburn-brown in a sort of exaggerated, wavy bouffant. But, other than that, she seemed the same, only a little more determined, a little more resolute. She looked exuberant and hopeful but, though I rejoiced in her stubbornness and respected her courage and the way she soldiered on, dark thoughts entered my head. We couldn't remain in this fantasy world. She was old, losing her memory. She might even have Alzheimer's. She was a woman in retrograde. We *had* to do something. She couldn't run a business at her age.

I couldn't fake it nor deny it.

Whatever she was planning, I had to shut it down. Blue had to go home.

CHAPTER 9

*I*t was hot as we crossed the street, Blue with her chin up, a bounce to her step.

"We're going to have a party," she said. "We'll invite the friends of Odessa. She'll give us a list. She'll get them to come. And we'll invite Alejandro's friends. And Evandro's and Otavio's. We'll get everybody to come. They'll get to know each other. My family, the Lebanese, the Latinos, the Blacks. Odessa, she'll help."

Odessa was at her desk, scribbling on a notepad. She looked up.

"Something needs to be done." Blue leaned over the desk, looking at Odessa. "We can't let this continue. It has to be dealt with. And I have a plan. I'd like your advice. What about if we have a grand-opening party at my café and invite the folks who come to your Center? You must know everybody. It'll be a double-whammy: a grand opening party on the occasion of my birthday. It'll not only be a neighborhood affair, but a city-wide celebration with all three groups represented, the African-Americans, Latinos, and, of course, the Lebanese. In a way, it'll be a return to the old days, back when everybody lived and worked on Oretha Castle Haley Boulevard."

She waited for Odessa.

"Sit down," Odessa instructed, putting down her pen. "A party for African-Americans and Latinos... together? And Lebanese?"

"Why..." Blue settled in a chair, "originally my thought was for a gathering of Lebanese. But in light of recent events... when you consider everything..." She got up and began pacing. "With all this going on... I thought it'd be nice to include African-Americans and Latinos."

Odessa's mouth hung open.

Blue hurried on. "I mean, I haven't thought it out completely. I guess I haven't thought it out at all. That's why I've come to you. I know we can't just sit around and ignore the animosity. We must *do* something. This is not acceptable. And it must be done *now*. Before things get out of hand. We have to confront it. We could have a party for African-Americans and Latinos to get to know each other. That's extremely important. Or, invite everybody, African-Americans, Latinos, and the group for which I built the café, the Lebanese." She looked at Odessa. "Honey, I don't know what to do. I'm asking *you* for help. What do you think?"

Odessa sighed. "That's a hard one..."

"Blue," I interceded, "can't we think this over? First of all," I hesitated, knowing this wasn't going to be pretty, "do you think these groups would get along?" I waited before continuing. "Let me put it another way. They all have their different customs and ways of doing things. I don't think they're familiar with each other. It might be... *uncomfortable*."

"It's a *party*," Blue objected. "Maybe it's time they *did* intermingle. With all we've been through, the storm and all, wouldn't you think people might find a way of looking beyond the surface?"

"The world doesn't work that way. It sounds nice, but let's be real."

"What are you saying?" Odessa eyed me.

I turned to Blue. "I don't mean to shock anyone." I slipped into a chair. "But African-Americans and Lebanese-Americans *together*? In the era in which you and I lived, Blue, Blacks were the maids in our families. Aunt Marcia had Magnolia, Mama had Reatha, you had Blondeva—"

"Jamila, oh my God—!"

"Now, let me go on. I'm just stating a fact. Even today in this city, you don't see the two races intermingling. Even in nightclubs, you don't see an even distribution. There are always hundreds of one and hardly any of the other. Why, I took a streetcar to Congo Square one Sunday to hear a concert of gospel choirs from the various Catholic churches, and out of the hundreds of folks present, I was among a handful of Whites. All the rest were Black. Maybe it was just the Black churches putting on the concert, I don't know. All I know is that the only Whites I saw were the retired archbishop and a Congressman who wasn't even White—he was from Saigon. And he was only there to get re-elected."

"Please, you're being rude—"

"All I'm saying, I don't see any real socializing among the races in this town. Maybe New York. Or Chicago. But here? Let's be *real*. Blacks are heads of city government and have lots of important jobs. But do you see *friendships* forming? There was a story in the paper the other day about how Councilman Sammy Feldstein decided against running for mayor because the city's 67% Black population doesn't usually vote for Whites. He didn't think he'd get enough Black votes to win an election. You think I'm out of line? They don't even see each other as *people*. What I'm saying— and I don't wish to offend—but if you're trying to get Blacks and Whites together, this party's going to be a bust."

"I'm not offended," Odessa sighed.

She pressed the end of her pen against the corner of her mouth. "But why does everything have to be the way it was? Besides, how true was it back in the early part of the twentieth century when everybody mingled on Oretha Castle? Oh, I know it wasn't named that then. It was Dryades Street. But can you imagine Black merchants and Jews and Italians working together side by side six days a week and not forming friendships? I can't. And what about the immigrants living along the street? Surely they got along. Good grief, even socialized. If they can, so can we." She leaned in, looking hard at me.

"I don't mean to change the subject," I said, "but who was Oretha Castle?"

"What do you mean?"

"The person the street's named for—who was she?"

"An activist." Odessa sat back. "Back in 1960, Oretha Castle was only twenty years old when she was arrested for sitting at the Whites-only lunch counter at the McCrory's five-and-dime on Canal. She was there with three friends. All four got arrested. They charged her with criminal mischief. The case went all the way to the U.S. Supreme Court."

"And...?"

"In '63, the high court threw out their arrests."

"Well, I hate to bring it up," I said, "but what about the Latinos and Blacks?"

"What about them?"

"How are they going to mix at a party?"

"Now," Odessa pondered, "that's another story."

I turned to Blue, who was cringing.

"Blue," Odessa said, "sit down. You're making me nervous." Odessa turned to me. "I can see what you're saying. Being at the same party, it might backfire. To be perfectly realistic, it might be more helpful to have them sit around a table and talk about their grievances. So they can understand each other's situation. At a party where there's loud music and no chance for real talk, with tempers flaring and booze, it might make for trouble."

"But I won't let it," Blue flared. Flushed, she turned to Odessa. "We'll make it so everybody has a lovely time—we'll be having too much fun for anything to go wrong. And let me tell you something else"—there was fire in her eyes— "they're going to dance together..."

We waited for something else, something important or profound, but that was all there was. The fire was still burning when Blue stuck out her bottom lip. "African-American, Latino, Lebanese," she mumbled, "they're going to dance together."

"Are we sending out invites?" I decided to change the subject. "Are we going to announce the theme up front? That this is to be a party for Lebanese-Americans and African-Americans and Latinos to... sort of... I mean, what's the reason we're giving for inviting these particular groups?"

"You're making it too *complicated*." Odessa threw up her hands. "It's a party, we're inviting them, and that's all they need to know. And that it's the grand opening and Blue's birthday. How old will you be, baby?"

Blue opened her mouth, but silence followed. Her eyes went dull then fear crept in.

"Eighty-two," I hastened to help. Odessa and I exchanged glances.

"And what day did you say it'd be?"

Blue blushed. "Oh my..."

"December 10th," I volunteered.

Odessa studied her. "I'll bake a doberge cake," she said, taking Blue's hand in hers. "We'll just send out the invites and see who comes. Let's not bust our asses worrying and making things too complicated."

"But we really need to *plan*," I urged. "What kind of food —Arabic, soul, Mexican?—what bands to hire. Fredy Omar's a friend of Alejandro and the Latin king around here. He plays Latin jazz, meringue, salsa—he'll draw a good crowd—"

"—and ruler of my heart, queen of soul, Irma Thomas—" Odessa lifted up her thumb. "She's a friend of mine. She'll sing a couple songs, get the party rolling."

"Now we're getting *somewhere*." Blue seemed revived. "Jamila, let's go home, plan the details, and come back for Odessa's input. Or, Odessa, would you like to be in on all the planning, darlin'?"

"Go, baby!" Odessa's eyes twinkled. "Give it your best shot. Do the heavy planning and come back in a few days. We'll go over it then."

Blue trotted around the desk and gave Odessa a big hug. She practically bounced out of the building and floated across the street.

"Hey," I said to Blue, "don't you think Alejandro should be in on this? He may have some ideas."

Blue followed me into the building.

~

*O*nce inside, she stopped and turned on me. Digging her fingers into her hips, she looked sternly at me. "Not many people," she fumed, "would have put up with what you said. Odessa's a precious angel. What she displayed over there was remarkable class. What on earth possessed you to say the things you did?"

"Since when," I shot back, "does being honest become a capital offense? Things have gotten out of hand. I'm sick to death of political correctness. It's time people told the truth—"

"Sometimes it's best not—"

"*Ah ha!* So you think what I said was true? Only you think I shouldn't have said it?"

"Absolutely not."

"Then you think what I said wasn't true, that Blacks and Whites get along like ice cream on apple pie, like French bread and seafood gumbo? Is that what you think?"

"*People are not food.* What I think is you make me tired." Blue suddenly looked old. "What you said was *unnecessary*." She rubbed her eyes and then gave me a withering look.

"Blue, don't you think we should be allowed to say what might be ugly, distorted, invalid, even *if we believe it,* so we can sort out what's real? That we shouldn't—"

"Talking about Magnolia working for Marcia," she cut me off. "And Blondeva for me. Jamila, *honestly...* how demeaning. And how it's the same today. Don't you remember the manners your mama taught you? You may have been the daughter of privilege, but they taught you to be kind."

Blue looked a little exhausted. It was rare to see her that way, and it made me kind of scared. But I wasn't going to back down.

"Let me tell you something!" I said. "I can't picture this scene. In a hundred million years, I'll never get what you're trying to—"

"How would you like it if someone demeaned *your* race?"

"I wasn't demeaning *anybody's...* All I was saying was, the Lebanese dress beautifully. They're well dressed and well-to-do and get their best china out and pretty much socialize with people they *know. They have things in common with people they know.* Can you honestly picture Lebanese at a party with Blacks they've never met? And what about the Blacks? They're used to their own friends, their own ways of having fun, and... Blue... this may sound cold... I hate like hell to say this, but I've *studied* people... I can't see what you're trying to—"

"We've gone through *hell* together," she stammered. "It wasn't just Whites who went through the storm. There's nobody on earth telling us we can't celebrate together. Who's telling us not to?"

Her expression was something I'll never forget. It shamed me into silence. I wanted to get it out in the open, that she was too old to run a business, her memory was going bad, that terrible things were going to happen unless she went back home and let her family take care of her.

And then I thought of something else. I thought about what we'd been through, the storm and evacuation, and how, for one moment in time, we were all together, clinging to a sinking ship. And what could be worse than to have no hope at all—no dreams at all. And then I didn't know what to think, didn't know what to say. And I decided to hold tight to the coattails of Blue's dreams—maybe that would get me through this. She looked around the room, giving off that befuddled look, as if she'd forgotten everything we'd talked about. And then she returned to her old self.

"Come on," she stammered, "let's do what we came to do."

CHAPTER 10

e barely made it through the front entrance without tripping over the piles of stuff: a transistor radio belonging to Otavio, silk flowers and tables and chairs meant for other rooms. In place of Diego Rivera or Frida Kahlo paintings, we were graced with the paintings of one Alejandro Cruz leaning against a wall, waiting to be hung, and on the floor, four-hundred-pound wrought-iron chandeliers that Alejandro had found in Mexico.

Other rooms were in similar disarray. It seemed unimaginable that we'd be opening in little more than a month, which was what Blue was expecting. And as we stumbled our way past the piles of stuff, something else caught my eye: the building looked Latino.

Ceramic masks, clay figurines, and wood carvings hung from walls. And every room that wasn't brick was painted a brazen color: cobalt blue, deep indigo, sunset crimson, blood orange.

The kitchen was emerald-green, the banisters bold green over an original mahogany staircase. A small bedroom painted gold with gold lighting fixtures. The library, mauve;

another room, terra cotta with green and brown window trim and terra cotta floor tiles; another, deep purple with pale green stained-glass windows; still another, purest white beneath a mauve ceiling and white fixtures.

On Blue's bedroom wall, a gigantic mural of Mexico City. Alejandro stood before it with paintbrush in hand. And dispersed here and there, a mesquite table, carved armoire, a Jacuzzi under a tin-tile ceiling. The ambiance was pure Latino—Alejandro's doings, of course—so that I wondered why Blue hadn't considered making this a gathering place for Latinos, a cultural center, primarily theirs, to thank them for all they'd done in resurrecting our dying town.

Nothing else made any sense.

Alejandro stood with his back to us, putting on the finishing touches. As we entered the room, he turned, and it was then that I realized he bore a striking resemblance to Meredith's twin brother, Michael. They had the same raven hair, the dark complexion, the soul-sensitive eyes. They both had a mysterious quality that reminded me of James Dean. But it was more than the physical resemblance. They had a similar way of dealing with life, pausing to see and hear and reflect before facing with great dignity whatever trouble lay ahead. They were both salt-of-the-earth people, emotionally fearless, it seemed to me, never balking at adversity, facing their destinies head-on.

Michael's was already known. He and his wife divorced when he was forty-five, and he spent the rest of his life trying to win her back before dying of a massive heart attack in his sleep the following year. Alejandro's was not known, of course, and I silently wished him a happy life. Seeing us, he put down his brush.

"What do you think, darlin'"—Blue bounced into the room, revived at seeing her favorite person—"if we invite that boy to our grand opening?"

"What boy?"

I rolled my eyes in Blue's direction, then turned to Alejandro. "The one you had the quarrel with," I said. "The one who called you all those names. The kid, Lennus, across the street. That wonderful, angelic child. She wants to invite him to our party."

"And his friends," Blue added eagerly. "It'll be a lovely way to show our goodwill."

"Blue," I said, looking around, "this place looks like a hacienda. Did you really mean to make it so? You've got Mexican talavera sinks in the *shusmas*, Guadalajara tile on the walls, cactus plants in terra-cotta pots, Mexican folk art everywhere. Did you have a change of heart?"

"A change of heart?"

"Are the Lebanese to be your only customers?" Alejandro wanted to know.

"I never thought of them as customers, darlin'. I more or less thought of them as guests."

"Surely the point is to welcome *people*," I said, "not necessarily just *Lebanese*. You look around, Mexico speaks to you."

Blue studied the room. "I let Alejandro do what he wanted. He has such good taste. It merely evolved into this."

"Why not welcome Latinos instead?" I argued, forgetting I needed to put a stop to this. Something had taken over, as if defeating the other side of me that wanted nothing to do with this. An excitement began to bloom. I saw the building, decorated as it was, for what it truly could be, and it was almost as if Blue's dream had for a moment become my own.

"They need a place to hang out," I insisted. "Many haven't lived in the city long and they're lonely, especially the migrants, with their families away, and they'd welcome a place to come. Besides, many live in Central City. You've got a built-in clientele."

Alejandro's eyes lit up.

"Honey," Blue approached the mural studiously, giving it her undivided attention. "I understand their loneliness. The Lebanese in the early 1900s lived like the Latino migrants do today. Five, ten men in a room. Working hard, saving their wages. They either sent it back home to their families in Lebanon or saved it for the return trip. My own father was only a boy when he arrived in this country."

"When was that?" Alejandro and I asked in unison.

"He came on a cargo steamer many, many years ago. The Turks were carrying on a religious war with the Christians, and the Christians were getting the worst of it. In Lebanon, in a suburban part of Beirut, there was a small Christian Maronite village called Harektahrek. This area was dominated by the Christian Maronites during the Ottoman Empire."

She paused before going on, "Most of the Christian Maronites were strong people but were persecuted by the Muslims, who forced them to submit to their religion. They used to call the Christians 'cockroaches.' They were not allowed to mix with them, not even to walk on the sidewalks. They had to wear dark black cloths, so they could be recognized as infidels.

"Daddy was the youngest of six siblings. One of his brothers, while defending himself, killed a high-ranking captain of the Ottoman Army. He was captured by the Turks. Daddy, with his older brothers, rescued him and they all went their separate ways, coming back to America, each on his own, so as not to be caught traveling together. My daddy landed in New York, knowing little English."

"How did he end up in the Delta?" I asked.

"His eldest brother, Abdou, had come to American two years earlier. He'd been sending money back to his family in Lebanon. Daddy came to stay with him, ending up in Jeremiah. Together with Abdou, Daddy, who was only sixteen at the time, made his way by foot through the countryside. That's where they sold their piece goods. They'd each carry a case on their backs, a valise in their hands, and walk hundreds of miles. Later, Daddy and Uncle Abdou bought a horse and buggy and, years later with the money they saved, managed to own their own shop."

Blue glanced again at the mural before turning back to Alejandro. "Your people and mine have different skills, honey. The Lebanese were peddlers, the Latinos builders. But in many ways, they're the same. They work hard, they're good neighbors. Whatever they're given, they give back a hundredfold."

While Blue and Alejandro were talking, my thoughts turned to my own father. He and Uncle Imad were partners in the family business, which had been started by their parents. Daddy's father, *Jiddy* Najeeb, was forced to leave Beirut because of persecution from the Muslims. His mother, *Sitty* Yasmine, lived in Schweir, Lebanon, but fled for the same reason. They met in New Orleans, and *Sitty*, a member of the Greek Orthodox church, converted to Catholicism and married *Jiddy* in St. Louis Cathedral. They started a wholesale dry-goods business somewhere in the Quarter.

It wasn't a success. *Jiddy* was too soft-hearted. He gave credit much too generously, and his buyers rarely paid him. *Sitty* convinced him they'd make a better living in Harbortown, Mississippi, and so when Uncle Imad was one and Daddy three, *Sitty* and *Jiddy* left New Orleans and started over in Harbortown. They sold linens and lace from a horse and buggy.

When *Jiddy* died—young, I'm told—*Sitty* ran the business alone. She was an amazing businesswoman. The business prospered. When Daddy and Uncle Imad grew older, they developed commercial properties along the Mississippi Coast, Uncle Imad working out of his men's toggery, Daddy out of his department store. And so for six days a week for more than half a century, they got in their car after breakfast and drove downtown to work, walked to their separate stores, got back in the car after six, headed home in time for supper, and started the process all over the next day.

"And so it's settled?" I interrupted Blue, still chatting away with Alejandro. "The café will be for Latinos?"

"I suppose," she said quietly. "Nobody told me who to invite. I suppose it can be for them."

"If this is what you want." Alejandro moved closer to Blue, putting an arm around her shoulder. "You no look happy. You must do what you must do. You spend plenty money. If you want Lebanese, we no argue."

"It's just that," Blue pondered, "I thought if it was to be my destiny to create all of this, I'd create it for my family—to honor them. I wasn't sure who the café was meant for. Mary never told me. I just thought about my New Years' parties, the memories of those wonderful years, and I wanted them to live on."

Blue lowered her head. She must have been thinking about her life so many years ago, for when she suddenly opened her eyes, they were shiny and wet.

She put a finger under her eye and flicked off a tear, her voice took on a hard quality. "The interior wasn't designed to be Lebanese," she said. "I have no idea what a Lebanese interior looks like, other than having a mural with belly dancers and camels. The Lebanese I know are Americanized. Their homes are stylish but in a personal way, not a Lebanese way, whatever that is. It's the food that's distinctive, and I'm very good at that. So my café was to be known for its Arabic food and welcoming spirit, not its decor. Anything lovely will do. And Alejandro came up with the loveliest ideas. How could I not be pleased? I think what he has created is truly a work of art."

"Jamila right," Alejandro said firmly. "The building no look Lebanese. But you do what you must do. Invite the United Nations, if you like. You boss lady, no need our advice."

"I see what she's saying. The Latinos need their place. But I'm not ready to give up my Lebanese." Blue gave Alejandro a long look and her face filled with gratitude. "But you're *wrong*, darlin', I *do* need you. I couldn't have done any of this if it wasn't for you. You and Jamila. Why, I've been so busy I haven't even thought of a name."

"For the building?"

"I'm tired of calling it the 'building.'"

"If Latino," Alejandro offered, "I'd call it Café Guadalajara. What you call it for Lebanese?"

"In Lebanese villages, there was always an area that was the center of activity," Blue said. "They came together and argued, played cards, smoked the pipe. It was a public place. Jamila, can you remember what they call it?"

"Assaha," I said, remembering her old stories.

"Ah, yes, assaha! We'll call it Café Assaha!"

"Hey," I countered, "I don't want to put a damper on things. But if you're not sure who our customers will be, why not call it Café Internationale?"

Her eyes dulled. She was silent. The name wasn't to her liking.

"Why not let the party decide?" she said. "Whichever group comes in greater numbers, has the most fun, appreciates it the most, this will be theirs. We'll serve Arabic, soul and Mexican. Later, we'll narrow it down to one. And the name can be neutral: Dryades Street Café evokes the past. That's what we'll call it 'til we decide on something better."

"Wait a minute," I protested. "You can't just rename an establishment after a grand opening party. And you can't just remake a menu. They'll already be printed out. Things have got to be decided *before* we open."

"Then the name will be"—she caught her breath—"the Dryades Street Café. And our menu will be a smattering of everything: soul, Middle Eastern, Mexican. Later, depending on the situation, we'll make changes to accommodate whichever group."

I thought about it. The name Dryades sparked a hazy memory in my mind of something I'd learned some time ago, that dryads are supposed to be female spirits of nature who preside over the groves and forests. It amused me. Somehow, I could picture Blue's spirit presiding over the Boulevard and whoever came to eat her food.

Alejandro picked up his brush. He returned to his touch-ups, thinking we'd ended our conversation.

"One more thing," I said, tapping his shoulder. "Blue wants the grand opening party to be on December 10th. You think we'll be ready in time?"

"No!" he said, slapping the air with his brush. *"No way possible!* No have mixed occupancy permit by then. No have electricity on. No build handicap ramp by then. No hood for kitchen. No liquor license. No finish floors. No finish kitchen. No waitstaff. No... "

"Mama mia, take it easy—you'll liveaah longer!" Blue laughed.

"No way," he repeated, *"No possible way—"*

"We'll get it done," Blue said calmly. "On the night of my birthday party, we'll celebrate with family and friends in my beautiful new Café."

CHAPTER 11

*a*fter our talk, I was relieved to discover how sharp Blue's mind had been, relating the tale of her father, remembering as though it had happened yesterday.

But I reminded myself that old folks remember personal history even as their bodies grow weak and minds decay. And the optimistic insanity that came over me at the café began suddenly to cure itself. To say I was ambivalent about her plans was the mother of all understatements. Still, I permitted myself the illusion of rejoicing in the good that was, even allowing myself to believe, if only for a moment, I might be worrying needlessly, thinking Blue was drifting off.

There was nothing wrong with the indomitable Bahia Bechara Kaddoura Hamieh, I told myself, and so I concentrated on the details of getting the building finished. In the torpor of the days and weariness of nights, the men labored in a manic effort to do my aunt's bidding, getting the Dryades Street Café finished in time for the grand opening.

And that's when I discovered new reasons for concern. As the days pushed forward, my heart began to tear apart as forgetfulness settled over Blue like dust motes on an old piano.

I could deny it before, pretending it wasn't happening, because I'd been rooting for Blue and Oretha Castle Haley Boulevard. I guess I'd always been an entrepreneur at heart. It was in my blood, as it was in hers. In my heart, I wanted miracles, for the building, the Boulevard, the neighborhood, my aunt. There was a magnificent challenge ahead, and I wanted to be part of it—do what I could to help.

But in the succeeding days, the problems intensified.

In the beginning, shortly after buying the building, Blue went on a crusade: No more of this foolishness about not being able to speak English. After supper at my house, she'd invite the Brazilians over. There, using picture cards, or whatever she could lay her hands on, she'd embark on an hour's English lesson. It took me back to the old days when Blue sat with us children on the carpet in the center hall of her house and made a game of teaching us Arabic. We learned, *"bil mahrajan min-ghanni, wa min-urqus"*—"at the mahrajan we sing and dance"—or *"ana biHib rooH 'aa lubnan kul sini"*—"I like to go to Lebanon every year."

"Blue," Meredith fussed, "we're never gonna say these stupid things."

And so she began teaching us common phrases, like *"ya haram"*—poor thing—or *"sahtean"*—thank you, enjoy—or *"ana bahibbik"*—I love you.

Watching her with the Brazilians, I saw her teaching them with the same gusto she'd once used on us. But as the days journeyed on, Blue would forget simple words. She'd stammer and stutter, forgetting what she'd introduced them to only minutes before, and it was left up to me to take over the lesson, leaving Blue her shamed apologies.

She'd forget to close the gate at night, allowing Pelusa to run away. We'd drive through Central City, with me waiting in the car while Blue knocked on every door, asking, "Honey, have you seen my dog?" We'd drive all day long, posting signs on street poles, Blue insisting on putting my home address and our phone numbers on the signs for the whole world (and crooks) to see so that she could offer a fat reward. And this was the thing that got to me: Not only would she forget my contact numbers, she'd completely forget her own.

I couldn't ignore the implications. It raised enormous issues. As heartbreaking as it was to think about, I feared dementia had set in. One day, Blue would be helpless. Sally Ann would have no choice but to put her in a nursing home. And what about the building? We didn't call it the building anymore. We called it the Dryades Street Café. But in my mind, as exciting as our hope had been on the day she first named it, it had regressed into some worthless, inconvenient object—some burdensome, bothersome thing—not the great treasure we had created, the object of our massive pride, the work of art we had come to cherish. In my heart, I knew we'd have to get rid of it as our dear Blue deteriorated.

While all this was going on, me worrying myself to death about her, she refusing to let it get to her, she was in a tizzy to host as many parties as she could in practice for the main event. In the hectic days leading to the grand opening, Blue became the social butterfly she was put on this earth to be.

~

*G*rand Baroque. Silver goblets. Gold-rimmed china. Centerpiece of fruit. Candlesticks with ivory candles. I stood in the doorway, gazing into the Café. Smaller candles in every booth, fresh sweetheart roses in delicate vases. Gone was the clutter, things to be put away. A starry-lit room with booths by the left wall, the bar and bandstand by the right and, in the center of the room, small tables shoved together to form one long one, draped in ivory linen. I bent to take a peek at the gold-bordered name cards before each golden china plate when Blue hurried in. Heavy rouge, pale powder, bright-red lipstick, hair done in a salon. Her dress brought out her eyes.

"Blue, you look awesome!"

Alejandro and the Brazilians had completed the grueling task of getting the building ready. The city permits inspector had inspected the living quarters, and that went without a hitch. The electricity had been turned on, the sprinkler installed, the downstairs bathrooms made handicap-accessible, and an expensive handicap lift installed outside. Blue got her commercial license and liquor license, the tile laid, booths put in, the appliances installed, liquor ordered. The Latino cook hired. Now, Blue was stepping into the role of Oretha Castle's Elsa Maxwell.

Not everything went so well.

A week before, Blue had invited Lennus and his mom for supper. We dined in the upstairs library. It was an informal occasion for everyone to get to know each other. There was a tightness in the boy's face when he walked in with Alice to see the outstretched hands of Alejandro, Evandro and Otavio. Alice, taut herself, straining to be perfect, pressed her nervous hand against her son's shoulder to remind him of his manners. Everybody spoke at once.

Later, Blue chatted up the boy as he sat morosely throughout supper: "You're not eating, Lennus," she said sweetly. He hadn't even pretended to eat. "What are your favorite foods?" He stared coldly at her.

"Why, fried chicken," Alice rushed to answer. "He *loves* fried chicken... and he thinks French fries are to die for. Isn't that true, baby?"

An outraged arrogance, a smoldering condescending

presence, clung to Lennus. I sensed an explosion coming. Everybody gobbled down their food.

All except for Otavio. He sat, perplexed, a bit hurt, taking it personally, and in the most eloquent English I'd ever heard issue from his mouth, said, "The way you act, not good. We try to meet you halfway."

Lennus stood up, staring Otavio down, a smirk across his lips. He picked up his plate, flung it to the floor (I could sense his delight), the food splattering—baked fish, chickpeas, rice —an almost pathological hatred blazing in his eyes as he flung down his chair and lunged for the stairs to fast-foot it downstairs, cursing under his breath. We heard the front door slam.

One by one, emotions played upon Alice: horror, humiliation. She reached out to Blue. "Please forgive my son," she said. "He hasn't been himself since his daddy died. And sister... the storm... he was a hero..."

Hands clenching and unclenching, she got slowly to her knees. She began picking up broken shards. Awkwardly, she placed them on the table before scooping up the peas, folding them in a napkin, eyes brimming with emotion.

"You go to him," Blue said, getting down on her knees as well. "It's all right... you go to him. Never mind this. The boy needs you."

After that, Blue wasn't the same. She seemed reduced somehow, taking the rejection of the boy to heart, I suppose, sunk in her own morass. Perhaps she faced for the first time the oppressive bleakness of her situation. She may have blamed herself for her actions, doubting herself and facing reality as she came to realize the trap she had laid for herself. I saw her praying more often, working double-time on her rosary beads. She seemed increasingly tired, taking naps quite often. She'd always rested after her daily lunch. Alejandro would drive her to my place, where she'd rest for an hour, and then Alejandro would pick her up and bring her back to the building. But lying in bed happened more frequently now, as though she'd given up on life. Then, as quickly as it came, the deep depression lifted. She began planning another party.

It was peculiar. I didn't understand it, but I felt there was nothing I could do about anything. And, knowing that, I went along. Or maybe just took the easy way out.

~

*a*nd now, as I looked up from the gold-bordered name cards placed before each golden plate for her second party, I asked, "Blue, who's coming?"

I'd barely blurted out the question when she strutted away into the kitchen. I followed after her.

Nacho Valencia, the new cook, stood over the fryer.

"Is everything all right?" Blue asked.

"Yes, yes," Nacho answered.

"Is there anything I can do?"

"No, no."

Alejandro had recommended Nacho. Alejandro knew him vaguely as a former cook at the Pupuseria Divino Corazón on Belle Chase Highway. And through Alejandro, Blue met Elenita Magdalena Vargas and Lauriet Estela María Escudero, part-time waitresses at Restaurante Telamar. They all agreed to work for her.

Nacho was pouring oil into a fryer, looking like he didn't want to be bothered by us. Elenita, the new waitress, had her back to Nacho, placing sparkling wine glasses on a silver tray. She turned, smiled at us. But Nacho didn't even turn around. He was not exactly the friendly type. He seemed high-strung, bottled up. But Alejandro said he was a good cook and that was all Blue wanted to know.

The Café hadn't opened yet, the grand opening party being less than two weeks away. Apparently, this party was to be a dry run—a warm-up—for the great celebration we were all waiting for. Still, I had my suspicions about Nacho, some vague, creepy feeling.

Blue went to the fridge, took out a baking sheet.

"What's this?"

"Dauphine potatoes," she told me. "You mix water and butter and... and—" Flustered, shaking her head, she handed me a cookbook. "I can't recall the recipe but, here, darlin', you can read it."

It called for water, butter, and salt to be mixed in a pan, with flour added once the mixture had boiled. Eggs were then incorporated, followed by mashed potatoes, nutmeg, and pepper, all stirred into the chou paste. The mixture was shaped into one-inch balls and dropped into hot oil.

"Nacho's going to drop them in the oil, after he deep-fries the shrimp and crabs," she said.

"Shrimp and crab? So yummy! Why did you tell me to dress up?"

"I got the idea from an architect friend of mine."

She put the baking sheet on the counter, re-opened the fridge to check the other dishes: a green salad in a big wooden bowl and what looked like stuffed zucchini in yogurt sauce. The dish in Arabic was called *mihshi kousa b'lubban*. A heaping plate of *ma'mool*, a date-filled pastry, sat on a bottom shelf, wrapped in Saran.

"Holy cow, we're eating *good* tonight," I marveled. "What idea did you get from the architect?"

"He had a casual dinner." Her head vanished into the fridge. She was getting out the zucchini, putting it on the counter. "Or at least that's what we were expecting. It was a very long time ago when he lived out by the Back Bay. He invited everyone to dress casually, like we would dress for a picnic. And when we got there, we were served by waiters in tuxedos, carrying pheasant under glass. There was champagne, caviar. And we were entertained by the strains of a three-piece string ensemble. And here we were dressed in jeans."

"I didn't think you wore jeans."

"I bought a pair for the occasion."

"Yes, but—"

"And so," she smiled brightly, "I got the idea to do the reverse tonight. We'll all come dressed fancy. There'll be an elegant setting. But instead of something elaborate, we'll eat fun foods: soft shell crabs, shrimp, oysters. I thought it'd be creative, a little out of the ordinary." She looked anxiously to see what I thought. I watched Nacho scurrying about, harried, probably wishing we'd get the hell out of his kitchen. Elenita was breading shrimp. I wondered how the two got along. On top of the stove, a steaming pot of seafood gumbo, a smaller one with rice.

"Cool, Blue, way to go!"

The doorbell rang.

We were anticipating a wonderful night.

CHAPTER 12

*B*lue hurried to the door.

I scurried after her, catching a whiff of her perfume: gardenias. And there standing before us, her first invited guests—the Faysals: Saad, who was divorced, and his brother and sister-in-law, Melhem and Anna Marie. They were Lebanese family friends Blue had known for years. All the men in the Faysal family were ophthalmologists, the patriarch, Maurice Faysal, having performed the nation's first eye transplant. His sons, Saad and Melhem, were following in his esteemed career path.

Tears of joy welled in Blue's eyes as she gave each a hearty hug. *"Marhaba... welcome..."*

"Kaifa haloki... how are you?"

"Ana bekhair, shokran... I'm fine."

Standing behind them, May Hamieh Thomas, an elderly cousin who'd grown up with us in Harbortown. A widow in her late seventies, May lived in the Lake Front part of town. She was a sweet woman, and I liked her. Her late mother was a hero.

As the local legend goes, May's father had borrowed

money to invest in the stock market during the Great Depression. He lost everything in the crash. Shortly afterward, he died of a heart attack. That left May's mom—Zaina was her name—a widow with ten kids and another baby on the way—broke, in debt, with a small dry-goods store to run.

Shortly after the funeral, Zaina sat her children down around a long wooden table to explain the family situation, talking to them like grownups. All the menfolk in Harbortown had advised her to declare bankruptcy, saying it would be impossible to repay her debt alone. But she wasn't alone, Zaina insisted. There was someone who would help her. "Who?" they'd asked. She stared back at them in silence and, with finger pointing toward the sky, proclaimed with great earnestness: "Why, He will—God." She proceeded to tell her kids what their allowances would be, a quarter a week, something like that, and that she, with their help, would run the store and pay back every dime.

She did pay back every dime.

As she raised her family through the Depression, she gave secretly to the poor. Years later, long after Zaina had died, her youngest son invited us to a family gathering. As we congregated in his living room, he announced that a donor had given hundreds of thousands of dollars to be set up as an educational fund to help poor kids. It was to be called the Zaina Hamieh Charity Trust to honor her for all she'd done for his family during the years when they had nothing. The donor wished to remain anonymous.

Standing beside May in Blue's entranceway were May's daughter, Soraya, and Soraya's husband, Johnny. Johnny Chamoun had been a giant force in the city's economic recovery. He'd been selected by the mayor to serve on the Bring New Orleans Back Commission to come up with a master plan for rebuilding after the storm.

And behind them: May's other daughter, Isabel, and

Isabel's husband, Emile, the son of my mom's former boyfriend. Mama told me once that when she was seventeen years old and living in North Carolina, she'd attended a Lebanese convention in New Orleans and met Emile's father there. My father was also at that convention. Mama was chaperoned by her brothers. Emile's father and my father competed for Mama's affection. Mama's brothers convinced her to marry Daddy because he showered her (and them) with candy.

Blue escorted everyone in. I couldn't remember the last time I'd seen so many Lebanese gathered together in one room, and the room came alive with people. Saad Faysal paused to take in the high ceiling, the lighted candles. Blue rushed to put the music on: Tony Bennett, Michael Bublé. Johnny Chamoun, larger than life, taking over like the Lebanese men of an older generation, kidded and joked with everyone. He was the spitting image of his dad. I remembered May telling me that Johnny's dad, a 90-year-old movie theater magnate, once danced on a tabletop. I tried picturing that spry old man in a moment of intense exhilaration shaking his booty and stamping his feet between the salad bowls and wine glasses.

"You look beautiful tonight, Blue," Johnny marveled, acting as though he believed it, standing there admiring her, his arm around his wife's waist.

His wife, Soraya, had absinth-green eyes. She was gorgeous and funny. She once told a story. It was at one of her mother's parties. Soraya was telling the story of a trip she took with Johnny. They hadn't been married long. He woke one morning and said, "Let's go to Jamaica," and it was such a hastily planned trip that she didn't have much time to pack. Instead of taking a few pieces of jewelry, she threw in the entire jewelry box. The hotel they'd booked turned out to be a dud, and so they walked over to a better one, the bellhop following with their bags of luggage. The bellhop took a long time. When he finally arrived at the room and Soraya opened up her suitcase, she discovered her jewelry box missing.

"I said to Johnny, instead of losing all my jewelry, I'd rather he'd got caught having sex with someone."

"It smells wonderful," Anna Marie enthused, the smell of frying seafood commingling with her perfume. Elenita, shy but glowing, appeared with a tray of wine, and everyone took a glass. Johnny chatted her up in Spanish. Alejandro, Otavio and Evandro made their entrances, a bit timidly, and formally, but Johnny made them feel at home.

I watched Blue gazing in their direction from across the crowded room. It was a look that made me realize, probably for the first time, they were as much a part of her family as I. She seemed positively thrilled to see them. She introduced them to the Faysals, and the men shook hands, and even the Faysals, a dignified bunch, began to loosen up. It must have been from the many drinks Johnny poured for them.

And after we'd drunk our wine, Johnny made himself a vodka tonic, and scotch and soda for the Faysals. And after a few more drinks, when Tony Bennett began crooning, "*I left my heart in San Francisco...*" Johnny took Blue's hand and glided her across the dance floor. Both were quite tipsy.

They danced unselfconsciously, forgetting the rest of us. Blue's eyes were incandescent as if she were dancing with Uncle Imad at the now-defunct Broadwater Beach Hotel. Something special was in the air. A spirit had taken over. It must have compelled Alejandro, who was born to dance, to stand before Soraya, who didn't wait to be invited. She glided into his arms, and they danced gracefully and elegantly, May standing by the wall, smiling. Then Saad Faysal came to me, and Melhem to May, and Otavio to Isabel, and we all danced to Michael Bublé. And when the beautiful music stopped, in the dim glow of candlelight, we all sat down to dine.

A blast—the loudest, crudest, most unbearable piercing screaming urgency.

It did not cease. May shuddered. Soraya covered her ears. A scene I'll never forget, bracing against the intolerable. And in the midst of it all, voices:

"*Qué has hecho? Qué demonios has hecho?*"

"*Nada, no se...*"

"*Perra, lárgate, fuera de mi cocina.*"

I'd almost allowed myself to believe the night would end flawlessly, as in the glory days of Blue's parties. But now I couldn't fool myself. Alejandro was the first to rise. He dashed into the kitchen, followed by Johnny, Evandro, Otavio, and Emile, with the Faysal brothers not far behind.

It reminded me of the disaster that had taken place when I was a girl. It was Christmas at my parents' house, everybody eating in the formal dining room—Aunt Marcia's family, Uncle Imad's, and mine—when we happened to glance into the living room to see the Christmas tree on fire. The flames spread to the brocade curtains. The men leaped up, dashed to the tree in silence, the women in the opposite direction—to the back porch with the kids—my brother, Hab, grabbing the fire extinguisher, then blasting the tree while the men leaned it away from the curtains. I saw flames leaping at my younger brother. The leaning tree inched dangerously close to him, 'til Frankie, on the other side of me, halted its movement, and the fire was put out. We later learned its cause: a defective angel Mama had bought at Woolworths.

Along with the men, I ran into the kitchen. There, Elenita was crying. Nacho stood with feet apart, glaring at a powdery substance shooting down from bins under the stainless-steel hoods straight into the fryers. In them, the cooking seafood was now covered in powder, as were the potato balls in another fryer, the gumbo and rice on the burners, the zucchini on the counter.

"*Dios mío, eres tontá, tontá.*"

Nacho lunged at Elenita. Saad Faysal made a move to stop him. He pressed forcefully against Nacho's chest. Nacho reared back and slugged him. It was a powerful blow, knocking Saad down. Saad put his hand over his nose, stunned, and when he looked down at his spreading palm, it was covered in blood. His brother rushed to his side. Alejandro and Johnny held back Nacho. The Brazilians grabbed both arms and dragged Nacho, bellowing, through the kitchen out to the back. They gave him a mighty shove and slammed the door behind him, and then the fire alarm stopped.

"*I'm sorry,*" Blue cried out, her face sheet white as she grabbed some paper towels. "Is it broken?" She clung to Saad. "Oh, what can I do?" she wailed. "Are you all right? Let's go upstairs and have a look at this."

"And when you come down, Saad," Johnny called shakily, trying to make light of what had happened, "if you're all in one piece, my friend, I'm taking us out to supper."

"I'm so *sorry,*" Blue shouted, entwining her arm in Saad's, rushing him to the stairs. She looked back at Johnny. "I insist." She stood erect, her face turning crimson. "You are all my guests tonight. Dinner will be on me." She spoke dramatically, with great rectitude, as she always did when something terrible happened, her high-pitched quivering voice striving to sound natural.

"I'm perfectly fine," Saad said, embarrassed. "*I'll* be the one to treat."

Johnny turned to Elenita and spoke to her in Spanish, and Elenita, her shoulders trembling, shook her head in reply. Later, a smile appeared on Johnny's face as he continued to speak to her, and finally, Elenita relaxed, nodding her head in acceptance of what he was offering. Soraya guided her to the bar, poured tequila into margarita glasses.

"She wanted to stay and clean up," Johnny told us. "I insisted she come with us."

Just then, Blue and the Faysal brothers descended the stairs. Blue led us to the door and opened it. A stranger appeared before us. He looked at least six feet, five, his face sunburnt, his long butterscotch hair tied back in a ponytail. He looked like a raffish surfer or some out-of-work basketball player, teeth brown or missing, rakehell, reeking of booze.

"Got anything to eat?" he begged, running his tongue over his lips. "Ain't had nothin' to eat in days."

"Nothing tonight, my friend." Protectively, Johnny moved in front of Blue. He reached into his pocket and handed him a wad of cash.

CHAPTER 13

We drove to Bayona, taking separate cars.

It was a five-star restaurant in a 200-year-old Creole cottage on Dauphine Street in the Quarter. It had a world-class chef, and the food was quite pricey. Johnny reached for the check at the same time Blue did, but he wouldn't let her pay. There was a fight with the Faysals as well. In the Lebanese tradition, it was considered an honor for a Lebanese man to pay the bills, a measure of his self-worth.

Many a fiery battle has been waged over a check and to take that privilege away would be a metaphorical slap in the face. Blue, gracious throughout dinner, pretending nothing untoward had happened, grew pale as we sipped our coffee and seemed to retreat into herself. Amid the noise and chatter, I was hoping no one noticed. She seemed lost in the car going home.

"Let's not clean up tonight," I said. "We'll do it in the morning."

She didn't answer. I patted her hand.

"You know, Blue, it was just something that happened. It wasn't to be helped."

"I know."

"They'll forget about it in time."

"It started out so nice. I don't suppose... they've ever had a night like this."

"You never know."

"I've lived a long time and never had a night like this."

"He had a hair-trigger temper," I said. "How do you suppose he got that way?"

"Hitting my guest, indeed. I'm glad the men were there. Poor... what was the name of the young girl?"

"Elenita."

"Poor... Elenita... I'm so sorry. No telling what might have happened."

We had dropped Elenita off—she lived on Spain Street in the Marigny—and were heading back to Oretha Castle.

"What did happen?" Blue muttered. "I'm so shocked by it all."

"She was trying to do too much," I said. "She was taking two garbage bags out at the same time. Trying to show Nacho what a good worker she was, I suppose. One of the bags must have caught the emergency fire handle that sounded the alarm. And that activated the fire-retardant power."

"It was," Blue's voice drifted off, "just one of those things. Lord knows what might have happened if we hadn't been there."

"If we hadn't been there," I joked, "there wouldn't have been a party."

"To the girl, I mean. To the waitress, the darlin' girl..."

"I'd like to get Nacho and Lennus in a room together, see who makes it out alive."

Blue was in no mood for humor.

"And that homeless man..." I shuddered, remembering the beggar at the door.

Blue nodded numbly.

"They're encroaching," I warned, "closer and closer into our block. Soon they'll be sleeping on the sidewalk in front of our Café."

"People are so poor. That must be why I'm here..."

"What did you say, Blue?"

"Nothing."

"You said something. What was it?"

"It wasn't anything."

"I've been meaning to bring this up. Now is as good a time as any. You seem to be forgetting things a lot. Are you aware of that?"

"Old folks do..." She picked up her purse, laid it in her lap. "... From time to time." She turned to look out the side window.

"Are you sure you're up to this?"

"I don't know what you mean."

"Running the Dryades Street Café."

She cocked her head in bewilderment.

"There are so many details. So many things to do." I struggled for the right words, not wanting to hurt her feelings but determined to state the truth. "Blue... there's something *wrong* with your *memory*."

"Don't you think I know?" In the shadows of the car, I could see the pain those words had caused. She flashed me a brave smile. Her face twitched; she turned away, forlornly looking out the window. As I looked where she looked, I almost crashed into the car ahead. We were passing a public park. A young woman, wasted, tattoos running down her arms, moving as if she were stoned, got out of a ratty junk heap of a jalopy parked on the street and made her way into the park. As she headed toward an oak tree, I sensed what was coming. Sure enough, before she made her way behind the tree, she pulled down her jean shorts and exposed her naked butt.

Blue looked right through her.

"Mother Mary knows it too," she murmured. "That's why she told me to make a gathering place. No later than my next birthday."

"That was one detail you forgot to mention."

"No need to... at the time."

"Are you sure you aren't imagining it? I don't mean to doubt what you heard but what exactly did Mary say?"

"I don't recall."

"Why do you think she'd say that, Blue?"

"I have to believe she knew."

"Knew what?"

She never answered.

She didn't want to talk anymore. Presently, we were on Decatur Street, moving past the bustling French Market. Crowds of tourists rambled past the produce stands. Many cars moved ahead of us, the drivers gawking, looking for a place to park, out to party on a Friday night, and we were barely moving past Central Grocery where we always bought our muffuletta sandwiches. Just when I thought our conversation was over, she said, "There are things I remember. Do you remember the spruce tree I decorated for Christmas?"

That was thirty years ago.

On that particular December, the handyman had chopped down a tree in front of Blue's backyard garage in Harbortown. Blue had decorated it for Christmas and invited me over to admire it. I'd just come home on college break.

"It was pitiful," I recalled, "nearly gray, the most awkward, uneven branches. It was the ugliest Christmas tree I've ever seen in my entire life. Not only in *my* life but in the whole history of the planet Earth."

"It wasn't that bad." She smiled. "Do you remember what we did afterwards—after I showed it to you?"

"Yeah, we went to Aunt Marcia's."

"She was sitting in the dining room in the dark all alone."

"You remember that, Blue?"

"Like yesterday, my love."

"She looked at me," I recalled, "and said, 'Honey, I've been in so much agony. I have suffered such excruciating pain.' And all I could think to say was how sorry I was. 'Aunt, I didn't know... Aunt, I'm so sorry—'"

"She had been walking to the bathroom and had a black-out," Blue remembered. "The next thing she knew, she was lying in the tub. There was no water in the tub, and she called Magnolia for help."

"Her eyes looked like black marbles, large sacks under them," I said, "and I'll never forget the wrinkles. I looked at her for the longest time. I wanted to remember her forever, the hawkish nose, the soft white wisps of hair. So frail—poor Aunt—so grateful we'd come to visit."

"Do you remember what we did later?"

I thought about it. "We went back to your house," I said. "Sat on your settee in the formal living room to look at that catastrophe of a Christmas tree. Then you got out a portable radio with a cassette player inside and slid in a cassette, and we listened to MaryLynn."

MaryLynn A-Baki, my cousin from Mobile, had an amazing voice. She'd performed in a Christmas concert the previous year and taped it and given a cassette to Blue.

Blue's voice, quietly passionate, surrendered to the moment.

"You and I sat inches apart," she said, "listening to *Noel*. It was a very special time for me. There you were, back from college, if only for a few days. It was Christmas, we were listening to MaryLynn, and I felt so deeply moved. She'd begun the *Ave Maria* and we sat very still together. Her voice stunned me with its power, the timing so precise. And yet," her voice drifted off, "when it came to the moving part, it was fragile in its glory, a soul pushing through." She was silent and then she turned to me. "Do you remember, darlin'?"

"Yes... but how did *you* remember?"

She faced the front of the car, gazing at the car ahead. "And then..."—her voice lifted—"everything combined, the power, strength, and glory, and you and I just looked at each other, catching the miracle of what we heard, and then that moment passed."

"Don't you think it strange, Blue? After all these years, wouldn't you think we would forget?"

"Oh *no*, my love. Moments like that don't happen every day."

Her fingers moved toward her lips. A longing in her eyes, a sharp, exquisite pain. "It all went so quickly, and now it's almost over..." She paused and then considered,

"... the way life is almost over. Before you can blink an eye..."

"And the Café?"

"I beg your pardon?"

"The Dryades Street Café?"

She seemed fragile, not comprehending. And then it dawned on her what I was getting at. "It has to be done...," she said, taking a hanky from her purse. It half vanished in her folded hand. "I've been given this to do. You'll help me, won't you? You won't leave it for me to do alone?"

~

I stayed with her that night. We'd planned my sleepover in advance, on this, the first night she was to stay upstairs. It was to be a joyous occasion, a celebration with her friends before her official first night in the building. I told her I'd be glad to stay, honored to keep her company. But the night had turned into a horror, and so we dragged our bodies upstairs, ignoring the broken glasses, shattered dishes, and the grease splattered all over the kitchen floor. Silently, we made our way to our separate rooms and collapsed in our beds.

That night I dreamed about a closet, the emptiest closet I'd ever known. It was cedar—so vividly cedar I could smell it in my dream. When I awoke, sometime past four o'clock, that was all I could think about. How odd I'd dreamed about an empty closet, and how real was that dream.

In the dream, I'd been in the next room, staring at it from my childhood bedroom. And I began to be aware that what I'd been dreaming about was the closet in my parents' master bedroom. Their bedroom was on the second floor and, if you looked out beyond the windows past the balcony, you could see the blue-grey waters of the Mississippi Sound. That room was cedar-paneled, just as their closet was.

When Mama was alive, the closet had been crammed with all her clothes, her beautiful furs and beaded evening gowns, the casual dresses that had always fascinated me, a symbol of all that was exciting: the fun we children had running wild at the grown-up parties, the feasts, the myriad celebrations. But in my dream, that closet was empty, as were the lonely grounds where our house once stood.

I got up. It was five in the morning. I tiptoed from my room to Blue's, past where she was sleeping, and stood on the gallery outside her room, looking down on the silent street. The sky was pink and indigo, with a silver sliver of a moon. I felt an excitement where I stood in the presence of God without a waking soul around, whispering to empty buildings: *You must think of your lives, if it is thinkable to think, running back to your lives in the high-ceilinged dignity of the consecrated rooms, awakening in disbelief to nothingness and no one.*

I stepped back inside, pulled down the window. Blue was still sleeping.

CHAPTER 14

*O*n a Sunday soon after, in the cold, harsh light of day, reality set in.

I'd driven to the Café to pick Blue up to take her to yet another social occasion, scribbled in red ink in her heavily-marked social calendar, when it hit me once more how hopeless her situation was.

Except for some dazzling flashes of clarity, her memory was swiftly fading. There was a certain trickery to it: Some events in her distant past she could remember with stunning accuracy. But despite her most vigorous efforts, the recent memories we take for granted—what we eat in the morning, the errands run in the afternoon—would vanish before the day was up.

I knew Blue was no more capable of managing the book-keeping, ordering stock, training wait staff, and keeping up with payroll—the things you do when you run a business—than she was of recalling my cousins' names, paying Alejandro, or keeping the gate shut for the dog.

Things would inevitably get worse.

I didn't even want to think about what our family was cooking up. They hadn't called in quite a while. I could smell the rank decay of coming trickery. Or the way the buildings on Oretha Castle, driven insane by long neglect, were in collusion to spoil everything, all the good Blue would try to do. And rather than attribute my fears to paranoia, I preferred to think common sense had settled in, calling me to get with the program, find some way out of this sorry mess, get Blue out of it, too, before the sinkhole of good intentions swallowed us whole.

As I entered Oretha Castle, where it began at Calliope Street, I noticed the growing crowd of homeless folks sitting under the overpass. Alongside them, sofas, tents, couches, a festering shanty village. And then I saw a solitary figure in a wheelchair in front of St. John the Baptist Catholic Church, smacking gum, watching the street, goofily waving at passing motorists. A woman stood by a pole, talking to it. At the farther end of the block, a blue duffel bag and tennis shoes lay unguarded on the sidewalk in front of a vacant building. No one visible across the street outside the New Orleans Baptist Mission. But in the next block, a man sprawled on the grass, a plastic flask by his side, and fifty feet farther on, a slovenly woman lay on the grass beside some silver malt liquor cans. Two drifters talked beside a parked truck, one sitting on the curb, whiling away the hours—homeless, idle.

In the next block across the street, on Erato, sixty or so men and women lined up in front of Little Solid Rock Missionary Baptist Church, none older than forty, I guessed, waiting to be fed. A chain-link fence guarded the perimeter of the burnt-out school building, the structure undisturbed, untouched by human progress.

And in the next block, a building on the corner with a bright red-and-white sign sporting a large X across it and the

words: "N.O.F.D.—vacant structure placard." There wasn't a
soul on the street except for a woman in pink dress rounding
the corner to Martin Luther King Jr. Boulevard. A few cars
passed by. I shook my head, a growing hopelessness
spreading over me.

Not that anything looked sinister.

The sky was vast, the street wide. A feel of promise in the
air with so many handsome buildings linked side by side
along the vast stretch of the Boulevard. But there was also a
sense of languor, like a long, somnolent autumn day where
nothing much ever happens. And I thought of what Blue said
to Meredith, how she could picture this street bustling with
people (the ones with money in their pockets, no doubt)—"It
only takes one person to get things started, darlin'"—and
how she wanted to be part of it, be there to witness the
miracle.

I thought of all the years since the beginning of the
decline, back in the mid-60s, half a century earlier, and how
in all those years nothing much ever happened, the languor
and decay lingering, and how was Blue supposed to reverse
all that? How could one old lady move a gigantic monolith
with nothing on her side but a dream? I passed Terpsichore
and Euterpe and parked in front of the Café.

She stood waiting on the porch. "Let's hurry, darlin', or
we'll be late," she called out. She'd asked me to take her to a
cocktail party at the Lebanese Club near Bayou St. John.
Officially, it was named the Syrian Lebanese American Club
of New Orleans. She wore a crimson zebra-print silk dress, I
a black ruffle-sleeve dress.

She got in my car. We drove away. I parked on Mystery
Street. We entered a grey reception hall. A woman trotted
over. Her name was Salwa. She greeted us, escorted us
around, and introduced us to everyone. We headed toward a

tall, angular gent, slender and elongated. He stood in a corner, drinking a Manhattan. He was having a look around, his old eyes nearly popping out of his head when he spotted Blue sashaying toward him.

"Keefak—how are you, angel? It's been so long, my love!"

I recognized the man. He was Russell Kalify, the orchestra leader at the Broadwater Beach Hotel, but surely now retired. My mom and dad knew him. He lived in New Orleans and had a regular Friday night gig in the Blue Room of the Roosevelt, but every Saturday would drive the seventy-five miles to Harbortown to play the Broadwater Beach Hotel. In its heyday, Broadwater Beach was the Mississippi Coast's premier resort, but the new owners had shut its doors one month before Katrina, demolishing it to make room for upscale specialty shops, a pitiful trick life played on them.

Russell rushed toward Blue with outstretched welcoming arms. But when he saw her standing frozen, looking befuddled as he came forward, he instinctively backed away.

"Blue," I hastened. "This is Russell Kalify. You and Uncle Imad used to dance to his music at the Broadwater Beach Hotel. Practically every single Saturday night."

She gathered up her thoughts and smiled with gentle radiance. *"Mleeh, Ilhamdilla...,"* she greeted him, arms enfolding him. "Imad *loved* your music. And how is... your darling wife?"

"Sultana? She passed on."

"When?"

"After the storm."

"Oh, I'm so *sorry*, my love. God bless her precious heart. You know, Imad has been gone for years. This is..." She gestured my way but seemed suddenly panic-stricken, as if she'd forgotten who I was. Russell took all this in, catching the drift of what was happening, and threw me a knowing look.

"Jamila...," I said delicately. "I'm Jamila. Your niece."

Catching her mortification, I instantly turned to Russell. "Moawad was my dad."

"*Salaam.*" He threw his arms around me. "Why, you were just a little girl when I last saw Moawad and Naomi. Your daddy was a fabulous dancer."

Daddy wasn't so much a fabulous dancer as a jokester on the dance floor. He'd clown around, exaggerating his movements, having a grand ole time, and Mama, a partner in his high jinks, acting as though she delighted in his performance. He had the most wonderful sense of humor, cracking jokes at the dinner table whenever there was an admiring audience, and Mama, a comrade in that too, laughing, pretending she'd never before heard his jokes and what a clever man she'd married.

Daddy's eyes were droopy. They hid behind frame glasses. His nose was hawkish. He had grey hair, a slightly bald pate, big ears. He was five-feet-ten or so, getting thinner in his later years, pants drooping, voice gentile. Once, I heard a tape of William Faulkner delivering his Nobel Prize address and thought, "That's my Daddy's voice"—Southern, eloquent.

He was brilliant. Uncle Imad called him a business genius. Daddy once told me he'd been a candidate for a Rhodes scholarship in 1919 while a freshman at Ole Miss, but had to drop out of college because the doctor said his mom was dying. Daddy got a kick out of that. His mom outlived the doc, surviving past 105.

It's funny what one remembers. I was five. It was Daddy's birthday. My brothers and I were upstairs in his office. I'd given him a birthday gift. He took great delight in opening it,

VICKI SALLOUM

thanking me many times. It was a toothbrush. I don't recall the color, but he raved about that toothbrush, made a point of showing me where he would display it.

Shortly before he died, I spent the night with him in the hospital, sleeping on the couch. My brothers and I took turns, but that night it was my turn. He'd toss and turn, and I'd get up to see if he was all right, and he'd tell me, "Baby, go to sleep." He was worried I wasn't getting any sleep. In the morning, when Mama arrived, this is what he told her, "Naomi, Jamila is *faithful*." He only lived a few more days.

Eight months after he died, Uncle Imad dropped dead. Sally Ann, Meredith and Blue were with him in Blue's and Uncle Imad's kitchen. Uncle Imad had been hospitalized for a heart attack and was released the previous day. They buried Mama exactly a year from the day my daddy died. And Daddy's sister, Marcia, who lived to be 92, was buried on that same date, a decade later.

I left Blue alone with Russell. The guests and Club members were mostly old, but a few younger ones were also hanging out. The physical features of the younger guests— olive skin; dark hair; soulful, deep-brown eyes—made me smile, as though I'd been standing in front of a mirror gawking at my younger self. A few more guests arrived and Salwa, ever the attentive hostess, introduced me to the new arrivals: Joe Haddad and his wife, and two old spinsters, Pheado and Josephine Menasa.

I was bored, didn't have much in common with them, though I felt honored to be part of them—felt a special pride in my heritage. I had decided one day, after Blue had told Alejandro and me the story of her father, to learn about the land where my grandparents had been born.

After Blue had gone to bed that night, I went to my computer to look up the history of Lebanon. I learned that Lebanon was at the eastern edge of the Mediterranean Sea.

No bigger than the state of Connecticut, it bordered Syria to the north and east and Israel to the south. It was home to the ancient Phoenicians. Over the thousands of years of its existence, it'd been invaded or conquered many times, by the Persians, Greeks, Romans, Arabs, Crusaders, the Egyptians, and Ottoman Turks.

The 600 years of Roman rule, starting in 63 B.C., was supposed to have been its most peaceful time, while the 400 years of Ottoman Turk rule, starting in 1516, was by universal agreement its most stagnant. Eventually, Lebanon was put under the rule of France. In 1943, it became a free republic.

I once sat in a beauty salon reading an article in *Wine Spectator* in which a famous Lebanese winemaker was quoted as saying, "Lebanon—since its inception 10,000 years ago—has always had war." He went on: "You have to accept it. I never worry. For the last five years, I've told myself, be happy, be positive, be funny."

I remembered Daddy telling me about his mom. Coming from a village in Lebanon called the Shwayr, *Sitty* Yasmine had lived in America for over seventy-five years when her children, as a birthday gift, wanted to send her back to Lebanon for a brief visit with her family. She wouldn't go, Daddy told me. She declined the trip. She said, "If it was so good there, why would I come here?"

Blue chatted with Russell before mingling with the other guests. Before long, a circle gathered around her. I was impressed by that, since I'd never had Blue's talent for finding the fascinating side of people. And before the night was over, she'd made at least a dozen friends. She invited them to high tea at the Café the next day, an engagement already noted in her frenetic social calendar. Several days earlier, she'd invited some old Black women from a nursing home in Central City, folks she'd met following their performances in a musical at the Frederick Douglass Center.

High tea on Monday, at precisely three o'clock.

Though I should have known better by now, I was thinking the tea party would be a lovely, quaint affair.

Never did I imagine the catastrophe that would sear my soul forever.

CHAPTER 15

*T*he sky a melting blue.

Winds ruffled the elephant ears in my neighbor's garden across the street, their surfaces splashed with sunshine. A nip in the air, chill up the arm if one were foolish enough to wear short sleeves. It was a dazzling, chill-in-the-face, bustling kind of day, droning lawnmowers, buzzing saws, rolling streetcars, squawking birds. Shadows painted the underbellies of the oaks along St. Charles.

That morning, December 7th, Blue called before daybreak. She'd decided to drive herself to Harbortown. Her plan was to buy flowers and say prayers at the family graves.

"Absolutely not!" I told her. "You'll never make it there alive. Driving alone, yes, indeed!"

"Oh, hush up. Quit your worrying. I bought a used car yesterday. Alejandro came along. A '02 Chevy Impala, for $6995."

"Oh my God, you absolutely cannot drive a beat-up clunker on the interstate," I lectured. "You'll be chugging along in the middle of the high-flyers, and they'll cream you and leave you for dead. Besides, you'll never in a million years be able to find that cemetery—"

"I've been saying prayers at that cemetery since you were still in your mother's arms."

"Wait 'til the weekend. I'll take you. Wait 'til then—"

But she insisted on going that day.

I convinced her to let Alejandro drive her, saying I'd give him directions to the cemetery. She'd had a dream the night before, she said, and couldn't stop crying. In it, she was playing the piano in the living room of her beachfront home when she looked up. Surrounding her was everyone she loved—Imad, Nayla, Naomi, Moawad, Yasmine, Michael, Marcia, and Fayad—singing *Just a Closer Walk With Thee, Pass Me Not, O Gentle Savior, Precious Lord, Take My Hand*, and *I Want Jesus to Make Up My Dying Bed*. They were all there to sing with her, and she never wanted it to end—never wanted to wake up.

"But what about high tea?" I asked.

She promised she'd be back no later than two, in plenty of time to prepare for tea.

❧

I was approaching Oretha Castle at four in the afternoon on the day of the scheduled tea when I saw something running out from under the Café. I was arriving from the office, where I'd been working on the medical symposium. It had a fancy name, "The Dr. Eberhard Schmidt-Sommerfeld Memorial Symposium in Pediatric Inflammatory Bowel Diseases," and the eighteen invited speakers were coming from as far away as Germany, Israel, Chile, and Peru.

It was a great responsibility. I'd been arranging their hotel reservations, preparing the paperwork for their travel reimbursements, planning the program, applying for grants, organizing a speakers' dinner, soliciting booth participation from pharmaceutical companies, promoting the event, sending out invitations, registering attendees, and a lot of other things. All this weighed very heavily on me as I reluctantly left the office. Blue had wanted me to be there early to help welcome her invited guests. She was hurt when I said I couldn't come. Feeling guilty about it, I decided to make a late appearance, then drive back to the office to work late into the night.

I was in another brain zone, obsessing about details, when something odd sliced through my haze. I was nearly a block away when I realized what I was seeing: two men scrambling out from under the raised building. One leaped across the front yard, heading for the street. He collided with a shopping cart while trying to escape a vicious dog.

The cart careened into the fender of a parked BMW. The vicious dog was in attack mode, diving for the stranger's foot. The second man ran past him, trying to make his getaway. He stopped on a dime. I looked where he looked: two cops getting out of their patrol car, scrambling to draw their guns. He fled back from where he'd come, heading for the Café.

The second man passed his accomplice, who was in a frenzy, fighting off the dog. At first, I thought it must be some rabid animal loose on the street. And then I realized it was Pelusa. There was no pretense at being friendly. Her fangs sank into the man's foot, digging in while he screamed in pain. She wasn't inclined to let go as he dragged her to the runaway cart, then took something out of it and clobbered her over the head.

As Pelusa gave out a mighty yelp, the man staggered up the front steps only moments after his buddy. Panicked, Blue stood by the door, fingers digging into her temples, watching them go past her to disappear inside.

I parked behind the dented BMW, jumped out of my car, and ran into the Café. The scene was catastrophic: Russell Kalify standing in the middle of the room facing the back of the building; two elderly women lying on the floor, moaning; chairs overturned; china saucers shattered; tea in golden puddles; two spinsters from the Lebanese Club cowering near the bar. I saw the back of Joe Haddad as he followed Russell Kalify in a sort of old man's trot past the kitchen through the back door out into the yard. Voices rose behind me.

Two obese cops, gasping for breath, guns drawn, ignored the fallen ladies and hysterical spinsters as they hustled to the rear door, shouting.

"*Oh Lord... Jesus, have mercy...*" This was Blue's reedy voice. It could be heard amid their shouts.

As I ran after the cops, I saw Blue, kneeling.

"*... Darlin'... sweet darlin'... please tell me where it hurts...*"

She was bending over the old woman, who was favoring her right arm. The old woman looked to be at least eighty. Blue, on her hands and knees, began crawling toward the other guest, who was showing no signs of breathing. Blue picked up her hand to feel for a pulse and slapped her a few times before beginning CPR. She stopped when it became clear she didn't know what she was doing.

"*Honey, open your eyes. Open your eyes and speak to me—*"

I leaped down the back steps, following the cops. One of the intruders was lying on the grass, a snarling Pelusa on top of him. The last time we'd weighed Pelusa, she weighed at least one hundred pounds. It would be awfully hard to get up. They were at the farthest quadrant of the backyard, the distant part of the fence. Surely it had been their plan to make their leap to freedom, but Pelusa was having none of it.

Not only was her full weight planted on the man's chest, but the ankle of the other man was also clamped inside her jaw.

The man was beating her, the cops commanding him to stop, *put down that gawddamn pipe*, while Pelusa maintained her stance, unwavering, heroic, steadfast against the blows.

I vowed I'd give that dog a party if it was the last thing I ever did.

Both intruders looked horrified.

I ordered Pelusa to come to me. She'd always been my good buddy and instantly obeyed. As the men were being cuffed, I kissed and hugged Pelusa, saw she wasn't badly hurt, then put her on a leash and tied it to a rail. I hurried back inside. The second woman had her head on Blue's lap. She appeared to be revived, resting peacefully on Blue. I knelt down beside the other woman. She'd obviously broken an arm. The bone stuck out at a grotesque angle.

An ambulance arrived.

The cops hauled the thieves to Central Lockup, bringing the evidence along with them: the cart loaded with aluminum siding, old car batteries, a cast-iron sink, and copper pipe. Eventually, the room quieted. Blue looked overcome.

We sat among the ruins: upturned tables, broken chairs, and k'naafeh pastries and b'learwa splattered over the floor. Neither of us spoke. She cradled her face in her hands and looked down to survey the mess. We couldn't sit like this forever. I reached over and touched her hand, asking, "What do you want to do?"

I didn't think she heard me, so I repeated the question.

She looked foggy—deeply shaken.

"I'm going over there," she spoke hoarsely, "spend the night with her."

"The woman who stopped breathing? Where do you think they took her?"

"The public hospital. I asked Alejandro to check on her. She was there. She's okay. They took both of them there but... the other lady—"

"The one that broke her arm?"

"Yes. They put her arm in a brace. They're going to operate tomorrow."

"Isn't she too old for that?"

Blue looked shattered. "I'll let the doctors decide."

I cleared my throat. "I didn't mean what do you want to do now. I meant, what do you want to do about the Café?"

She seemed confused.

"I mean... this thing isn't working out. Surely you know that. What do you want to do about the Café?"

Blue hung her head. "I don't know if I want to do anything about it."

"You want to close it—shut it down?"

"I don't think that's in the works."

"I see."

We sat once more in silence. I took a deep breath, surveyed the ruins, and started picking up the broken pieces. I took them to the kitchen, dumping them in the trash. These were Blue's finest cups: delicate, gold-rimmed. I thought a lot of people didn't have such pretty things and went back to sit beside her. She hadn't moved. She reminded me of a discarded mannequin tossed into a dark alley. I spoke in my nicest tone.

"What's the use of seeing something through if it only hurts people?"

She flinched. "You're not giving it a *chance*."

"Blue," I protested loudly, "all the signs are there. The signs telling you this is a disaster. Maybe more than a hundred years ago, it might have worked out. You could have opened successfully then. But now? Blue, aren't you capable of seeing things the way they truly *are?* Thieves stealing stuff —my bike, your copper pipes—"

"—Didn't steal *mine.*"

"Stole *somebody's.* They were in the cart. The only reason they didn't steal *yours* was because Pelusa stopped them. If Pelusa hadn't gotten loose and chased them from under the building, you'd have to replace your pipes. The cops told me these thieves steal copper pipes from people's houses and churches and businesses and go sell them at sheet-metal recycling firms. But never mind that. And never mind the homeless folks sleeping all over the street. I had a dream the other night. I dreamed a bunch of homeless people were sleeping in my bed, piling on top of me in great big hulking heaps so I couldn't even breathe. One of these days, there's gonna be a thousand homeless folks crammed into this block, like a big circus come to town, sleeping in your door-way, spreading their sheets on the sidewalk, urinating in the bushes. Never mind even that. Don't you see what's happen-ing? Something far *worse.* People are getting *hurt.* That old woman almost died. Old folks have no business coming into this—"

"That's enough!" she said, shushing me.

"And you *know* that! You know what I'm telling you is true. Look at that other woman. The one who broke her arm. Eighty-year-olds who break bones sometimes *die*—"

"You don't have to go on!"

She put her hands over her ears. Defiantly, she removed them. "Can we continue this conversation later?"

"I'm gonna ask you one more time: Will you shut this place down?"

"That's not the thing to do."

"*Why?*"

"I've been given *orders.*"

To hell with your goddamn orders! Fuck your stupid orders.
But I kept my big mouth shut.

Her chin pushed forward. "Did you ever think, in your whole life, that there are things you have to do?" Gone was the defiance, replaced by a yearning to convince. "There are things you have to *do* because it's your *destiny* to do them?"

She was shaking. I thought she might be cold. I thought about going upstairs to get her a warm sweater but couldn't will myself to move.

"And you don't know what it is? You can't put it into words? But things keep pushing forward? And beyond the foolishness of it—because you have no idea what it's all about —you just keep pushing forward. Because... well... you *have* to? You've been given *orders*? Have you ever felt like that?"

I paused to consider the question.

It was an easy answer: "No."

It was surreal, the two of us, sitting amid broken cups. I could smell the sweet pastries scattered about the floor like broken strands of Mardi Gras beads.

Blue, looking intense, gazed past the open door to a building across the street, next to the Frederick Douglass Center. Her eyes grew misty, her voice breaking the gloom, and yet sounding so far away I had to strain to hear her.

"Maybe those windows over there," she murmured, "remind me of my family. Beyond them, everybody's gone. In those rooms where people walked, I can see your daddy and Imad greeting customers and telling jokes, and all the streets of Harbortown filled with busy shoppers—friends of Imad who grew up with him, becoming merchants and barbers and salesmen, come to buy their shirts and pants, whatever your daddy and Imad would sell them. And before you could snap a finger, gone... all gone." She stared, trancelike, at the building across the street, lips parted, almost stunned. "Before you take your next breath... *gone.*"

She leaned back and stared at the ceiling, though she wasn't really seeing anything.

"Like this street... all gone. Everybody..."

It wasn't self-pity in her voice—just clarity, tinged with wonder.

"Where did they go?" Her amazement was childlike. She seemed to sink into her deepest thoughts.

Then, suddenly, she came alive. She reached for my hand and squeezed it.

"Darlin', I want it back. Mary gave me the privilege of bringing it all back. And a mere bump in the road over a little bit of spilt tea is never going to stop me. Mary wants me to be strong. And I will not disappoint Her."

She looked across the street again, mesmerized by the broken glass in the windows of the derelict building in retrograde, squinting as if trying to see, imagining who'd been there to walk those floors. I did not interrupt her with the thought raging through my mind: *Somebody's gonna get killed.*

I knew what I was talking about. I'd gone to college in this city. I'd graduated from a small girls' Catholic college run by the Dominican nuns and taken a second-floor apartment on the dangerous side of Second Street. It was across St. Charles Avenue, on the lakeside. Second Street, on the riverside, was an upscale area, home to the Garden District with its multi-million-dollar mansions and private patrols to monitor crime. But where I lived, on the lakeside, was the mother of all urban horrors.

I didn't know it then. The block seemed innocent enough, though if you happened to glance into the next block, you'd see nothing but deteriorating houses. It was only after I'd moved in that I learned about the danger: men beaten unconscious on the sidewalk, homeowners robbed at gunpoint, cars vandalized, stolen. A retired merchant marine captain who was my neighbor in the Greek Revival apartment house where I lived had been robbed twice at gunpoint. Twice, my cars were stolen. Three times, I'd been mugged.

During one such mugging, I'd left my apartment at eleven at night to meet a friend at the Maple Leaf Bar, where the rhythm-and-blues pianist James Booker was playing. I'd walked out of my building to my car parked on the street. Across the street, two men were walking. One said to the other, "Get that dawg," and before I knew it, they were chasing after me. I ran behind my car with my hands over my eyes so I wouldn't see what was about to happen. A loud shout came through a window. A neighbor across the street was looking down from his second-story window, shaking his fist, bellowing at them, and the most amazing thing happened: the muggers ran away. Left me there. And because I had no sense, I threw my neighbor a big kiss, got in my car, and drove to the Maple Leaf.

The bar was nearly empty. My friend wasn't there. Practically the only people there were the bartender and Booker. Booker was seated on the piano bench, ranting at a few stragglers. Booker, a dope fiend who'd had too much dope that night, had chased everybody off. I went back to my car, drove home, and went to bed. Too many such incidents compelled my brothers to have a talk with me. They begged me to move out, saying if I stayed there much longer, somebody was gonna get killed.

"Somebody's gonna get *killed*," I said. "It's only a matter of time."

"Blessed Mother wouldn't have called on me if She didn't have a purpose."

Blue said it with absolute conviction, all-consuming faith, so unbending in her stubbornness and sacramental devotion, and getting so worked up about it, I was afraid she'd have a stroke.

After a pause, she said something else: "Mary speaks in different ways. Maybe you don't exactly hear a voice but your conscience tells you what to do, and you do what you are told."

"How's that?"

Blue didn't repeat it.

"Did Mary speak to you or not?"

"She did."

"Then are you sure?"

"About what?"

"About what you think She asked of you. She wasn't that specific."

Hunched over, voice flat, eyes betraying an uncertainty, she said, "We've been through this a thousand times. Let's not repeat it all over again."

"Okay," I shrugged, "but let me ask you something: Why would the Blessed Mother give a damn about Oretha Castle Haley Boulevard? Why wouldn't She care just as much about Harbortown, Mississippi? About the stretch of beachfront where all the houses were washed away? My family's, Meredith's, Sally Ann's—all the beautiful houses destroyed. Why would She want to save Oretha Castle and not East Beach in Harbortown? Or the starving people in Africa? Or the people of Iraq? Why would She pick *you* to be the savior? And why pick *here*?"

I thought my questions were worthy of an answer.

She looked back with imploring eyes. All around was the wreckage waiting to be picked up. We both took in the spectacle. She sighed. "I don't know."

It was simple and without retreat. A quiet acceptance at its core, a deep reservoir of hope, a mysterious, unquestioning faith.

It was all so clear to her.

I wished it were clear to me.

One simply obeyed. One had faith and one believed. And so it went. I didn't know how she managed it. Didn't know what was going on. Some grace had settled in. A strength from the holy trinity. She would carry on. We both would carry on. After all, this wasn't my problem. All I had to do was help. I'd never been nice to my mother and treated my father like a dog. In all my childhood years, I'd been a big, spoiled, selfish bitch, given everything and giving nothing. My parents loved me so much, and I treated them with contempt.

I remembered going off to practice-teach and Daddy writing me a bunch of letters. It was one of the few times I'd been away from home, and he wrote me every day. Two, three letters a day. Sometimes, they wouldn't say much; they'd just be this big, ugly chicken scrawl written in pencil on notebook paper. But it reminded me of a prayer.

Like someone who never forgets his prayers, who wants God to know he's thinking of Him. But those letters stopped coming after Daddy came to visit me. He went into the kitchen and saw a huge pile of his letters stacked up on the kitchen table. It was in Jeremiah, Mississippi. I was renting an apartment there, and the letters had not been opened. I'll never forget the look on his face. It wasn't a look of pain or hurt. It was a look of alertness and amazement, bafflement and understanding. Of an intelligence comprehending something stunning. And he never said a word about it. He just never wrote to me ever again.

I'd failed to honor him when he was alive, and now it was too late. And there was never a day after I matured and began to appreciate the implications of what I was that I didn't suffer from it. And so with this woman—my aunt—it had been my goal to help. So there'd be no regrets later.

But I no longer believed.

The only thing I did believe was that some calamity was on its way.

And then she got a call.

CHAPTER 16

*L*ennus was sitting on the curb at the corner of Felicity and Oretha Castle, lighting up a joint. It was a crystalline morning, and everyone could see him. Not that anyone was astir, not even a passing car. But somebody might pop up, even a cruising cop, and it disturbed me that he would be so careless as to take this kind of risk.

A lot of things disturbed me.

He was always alone. He had no friends. There were boys his age in the Center's youth group, but he never wanted anything to do with them. He was sixteen and never went to school, not that I could see. And nothing his mama told him seemed to make a bit of difference. Even the truant officer couldn't persuade him to go to school. He'd take his punishment—half a day in detention, a full day, whatever—and be back on the street the next day, smoking weed, getting in trouble.

He was a horrific kid, it seemed to me.

I kept thinking about the time he broke Blue's china plate, shocking Alejandro, Otavio, and Evandro and mortifying his mother. I kept thinking he must be some kind of brat the way he trash-talked Alejandro. And then I thought there must be some other name to describe this kind of behavior. And that's when I remembered that I wasn't so different from him when I was his age. Actually, I was much older, in my twenties, when I humiliated my mother the way he did Alice.

I was living in Miami, working as a teacher, and visiting the home of a married couple I knew. It was a long time ago. I can't recall the couple's name, only that the wife was the younger sister of a Lebanese friend of my older brother. Somehow, she'd found out I was living in Miami and invited me to Sunday lunch. My mother happened to be visiting me, so she invited my mother as well.

All of us ladies sat around the dining table—the hostess, her cousins, her Syrian mother-in-law—the men having retreated into the living room to smoke cigars after finishing our meal. The mother-in-law was talking about the Middle East crisis (this was in the 70s; there was some crisis going on), and she went on and on about how she hated the Jews, wouldn't stop berating them, getting her facts all mixed up, displaying her ignorance and stupidity.

My mother nodded congenially. I suspected she wasn't in the least familiar with the subject but being kind, appreciating their hospitality at having included us for lunch, let the mother-in-law rant on. I sat next to my mother, seething with resentment, as this woman denigrated the Jews. I had a Jewish boyfriend. He was a political reporter for a local paper, and I felt loyalty and disgust.

I never opened my mouth, kept my fury bottled up. But when she asked me what I thought, I told her I didn't agree with one damn thing she said. She looked at me with a cosmic arrogance, and it was like an atomic bomb going off. I spit out all the venom contained in my bitter soul as the

hostess and her cousins fled. I could see their horrified whis-
perings through the half-opened kitchen door, and it got
uglier and uglier with this woman and me, my sweet mother
trapped between the two of us.

I'll never forget how much I shamed her, how one could
not tell it from her demeanor, because she was used to me,
the loose cannon, savage daughter. And I'll never forget how
tired she looked, like a sick rabbit I once owned, lifeless and
fragile, 'til three days later the rabbit died. And soon after
returning home, Mama found out she had cancer.

I grew out of my rage, thank God. Never killed anyone,
went to prison. But I worried about Lennus. He was fright-
eningly like me. I'd led a privileged life, shielded from all
danger. But Lennus's potential for danger had no ceiling and
no bottom. There was no one to protect him, not on these
mean streets. Two days earlier, he'd got caught shoplifting, at
the Wal-Mart on Tchoupitoulas Street. He had taken a bottle
of cologne and aftershave to resell on the streets near Oretha
Castle. Days before, he'd got caught with crack cocaine.

He seemed to delight in being mean. Nothing gave him
more pleasure than smart-mouthing Alejandro, calling him a
shithead, asshole, motherfucker, spic. As big as he was and
small as Lennus was, Alejandro could have ripped him apart
and thrown away the pieces. But increasingly I came to
realize he saw the boy the way I did: one hundred and something pounds of oozing, gaping hurt. He sucked it up, took it
in stride, never reacting to the insults. I suspected it made the
problem worse.

Half the time, I hated the boy; the other half pitied him. I
was scared one day he'd go too far, sell drugs on the street—
if he hadn't already—get on somebody's bad side and get
stabbed, shot, or hauled off to juvenile prison. I read the
papers, knew how cheap life was. I saw enough pictures of
dead boys with crowds circling round them and mamas

wailing in the starless night about how their babies were no angels but didn't deserve to die the way they did. The crack cocaine incident particularly disturbed me. I decided to go have a talk with Alice.

She was sitting in her office, typing on a computer.

I stood in the doorway. "I'm worried about your son."

"Come in," she welcomed me, surprise animating her weary eyes.

She removed her hands from the keyboard, rested them on her knees. She wore a starched, brown cotton skirt and white button-down blouse, and her hair was tied in back. She was young, in her mid-thirties. She must have given birth to Lennus when she was about his age. There were framed photos on the walls and flowering plants on the surrounding shelves. There was a photo of a man beside her and a little girl, and a young Lennus. And everybody was smiling. *In better days*, I thought. Now, she looked like someone struggling to rebuild a life. On an ordinary day, she'd put her best foot forward, but in recent days, she had come undone. She never mentioned it, but it was clear: she was having problems with that boy.

"I saw him smoking pot on the street," I blurted out.

"I'm not surprised. He does it all the time."

"But they might lock him up."

"They've done that, too."

"Odessa caught him with crack the other day. Smoking it in one of the rooms. Blue told me, I'm sure Odessa told you. If that were the cops who'd caught him, he'd be up on serious charges. Can't you do something?"

"Won't listen to me. I talk to him constantly. Won't listen to anyone."

"What's wrong with him, Alice? I don't mean to mind your business, but I see him walking the streets all the time. He skips school. I mean, you know that... I don't have to tell you. One of these days, he'll get in serious trouble. He'll end up in real danger."

I had my nerve talking to her that way, an old maid who'd never changed a diaper, never had a child. She cupped her hands in her lap, avoiding me. And then she looked me straight in the eye.

"I appreciate your concern," she said. "Does me good to know someone cares."

"I feel like a busybody, but I'm worried about your son."

Voices filtered in from outside the office. I took the liberty of closing the door. Afterwards, I sat down. She seemed to want to talk.

"I pray for him."—her voice quivered—"I spend every waking hour trying to do my best for him. But... I think he's... I think my boy's..."

She couldn't finish what she had to say. Her face was changing colors. She picked up some papers and tried shuffling them around. She gave up, sank into her chair. If a human being can implode the way a dynamited building can, this would be what was happening. I yearned to go over and lift her, but she lifted herself up. A fierce pride emanated from her.

"My boy," she cried out, "is the smartest, most capable, most wonderful—" She looked ashamed, beseeching me. "I wish you could have known him..."

"... before the storm?"

"How did you know?"

"You said something the day he threw that tantrum. Something about his father."

And then she was telling me. Everybody has a Katrina story. Even I had a Katrina story. But his was like a killer whale compared to my shriveled-up tuna one.

They lived in a shotgun house on Tennessee Street in the Lower 9—he, his mother, father and twelve-year-old sister, Quenthasa. His little tomboy of a sister had broken her ribs the Friday before the storm, falling out of a high tree, and so evacuating wasn't an option. She'd be in too much pain moving about. And so the smartest thing they thought to do would be to stay home and keep her comfortable.

That Monday, August 29th, early, nobody slept. By dawn, Lennus and Quenthasa sat staring out the window. Alice watched her son's eyes grow wide after the Industrial Canal break sent a flood of water surging through the neighborhood, knocking down houses and sending them drifting down the street, the waters inexorably reaching their own. Alice screamed.

Lennus' dad, Elton, got out a ladder and climbed into the attic to lift Alice, but getting Quenthasa up wasn't easy. She cried out in pain during the slow, agonizing ascent.

They'd barely gotten her up when the waters surged in. Lennus managed to rip open a section of the roof and get his sister onto it, while Elton helped Alice. Then the house began crumbling—completely breaking apart, bobbing up and down, drifting through the street. Quenthasa screamed. Elton, stunned, clung helplessly. Lennus looked calm—amazingly, Alice thought—as the mighty winds screeched and moaned, and another house rammed into theirs.

Lennus got Quenthasa on the roof of the other house, got his mama there and his father. And that's when Quenthasa fell into the water, unable to hold on. Alice would never forget the look on her boy's face as he changed into a child again, watching his sister drift away. Shortly after, Elton fell in.

The two of them disappeared. Mama and son watched. Lennus was about to dive in when he saw Quenthasa's hand a distance from their floating roof. He shouted at Alice to stay low, hold on. He dove into the rising water. But the wind was too powerful. The water kept dragging him down, with Alice screaming, *"Baby, save yourself..."*

He never could have done it on his own.

Part of a splintered house floated into view. Lennus grabbed it, held on, and managed to get back to the roof. He reached for Alice, shielding her from the wind, and they never saw Elton or Quenthasa after that. They stayed holding on throughout the morning. As the storm gradually weakened, a rescue boat arrived. They ended up at the Superdome and, later, boarded Bus #729 for the 530-mile trip to Dallas.

It took eighteen hours to get there. They were housed in what had once been a minimum-security prison. Alice found a place to live, on the fringes of the city, and Lennus made sure she was settled in before hightailing it back to the Lower 9. What he did after that, she never knew. Where he slept, she never knew. Eating what? Doing what? He never would tell. He never talked about those days following her return. Always an independent sort, he was a stranger to her now.

Before their world collapsed, he did some good—halfway, at least—joining the school band, playing the drums, and making straight As in school. He never had to study. He got into mischief; he was no angel, after all—stealing whiskey, going on joyrides—but nothing major. His dad had always been there to straighten him out whenever he got into trouble.

Now, there was nothing. And he wouldn't listen. It seemed that ever since Katrina, his attitude had completely changed—one big fat chip on his shoulder.

Words once held back now spilled from Alice's mouth: "I told him, 'Lennus, no one's to blame. You can't go 'round hating people.' He said, 'They wouldn't let rich people drown.' I said, 'We were the ones who decided to stay. When something like this happens, it's on you. On me. You stand tall and do your part and be strong and responsible—do good for people, don't wait for them to do for you.' I said, 'Lennus, there was lots of folks died that day. It wasn't just our family. You have to go on living, son, try to get through it. You have to try, baby. You can't give up.'"

That's what he did. Lennus gave up.

"He wouldn't tell me, but I knew," Alice went on. "It had everything to do with his sister. He'd always protected his baby sister. It was born in him to protect her. And seeing her go down..." She shuddered. "And his daddy," she moaned, looking tearfully away, "he'd been injured on the job not long before that, so he couldn't hold on—his hand was too weak, and I think Lennus blamed himself for not doing enough to save him. I know my boy. He thought their going down was his fault. He'll live with that forever. He won't talk about either of them."

Tears streamed down her face. "It was just our bad luck. Our *terrible* bad luck."

Alice turned back to her typing. I got up and left the room. But I couldn't get it out of my mind. I saw him differently that day, just as I'd seen the homeless people differently after talking with Blue. I'd asked Blue one time to tell me if I had a bad attitude.

She said, "I don't think you have a bad attitude."

I said, "No, wait. I want to tell you something first. And after I tell you, I want you to tell me if I have a bad attitude. This is what I want to tell you: I see these homeless folks on Oretha Castle. Most of them look healthy. And I wonder why they don't get jobs. And I judge them for it. I think they're slackers, shiftless. Do you think I have a bad attitude?"

She thought about it. "I don't think your thoughts are that unusual. The only thing bad is that you judge them for it.

Many of them are able-bodied. But the problem's in their heads. They're depressed."

"A mental illness?"

"Yes, I guess you could call it that. Their spirits are broken. They've lost faith in themselves. That's why they need our help."

I saw them differently after that, just as I did the boy. I left Alice and walked out to the street, where Lennus was finishing up a joint.

"Hey, pal," I greeted him, "aren't you scared of getting caught?"

He looked at me like I was stupid, as though standing on a roof above the floodwaters didn't scare him, why would he be scared now?

"I want to take you somewhere," I said impulsively. "Somewhere nice to eat."

He looked like I was nuts.

"C'mon. No kidding."

He held the joint between two fingers, looking bemused and curious. He decided to play along. "Where the fuck you wanna take me?"

"Anywhere you want to go."

He didn't answer. I suggested Camellia Grill.

"What do you think?"

It was a popular diner, where all the college kids chowed down, and I wanted to give him a nice experience.

He paused, took a slow drag, looking bored, and said, "I don't give a shit."

"Well," I said, "would you rather go someplace else?"

"Don't wanna go no place with you."

"You'd rather sit on this curb doing nothing all day?"

He thought about it, took another hit, and shrugged off my sarcasm.

I said, "How about it...?" before it dawned on me why

148

would a kid want to spend the day with me? I was only doing this to assuage my Katrina guilt.

And as I was about to leave because I surely could take a hint, he called out, "I know where you can take me."

"Where?"

He didn't answer. He got up. Took his time coming over to me and whispered in my ear.

"Oh," I groaned, "no problem."

$\sim$

*B*ut it really *was* a problem. I was driving Lennus over the Industrial Canal Bridge on our way to the Lower 9. I'd told him it wasn't a problem, but, in truth, I was scared to death. I'd done it once before with Blue and didn't like it. There was something about the isolation and sense of danger and foreignness, a feeling that anything could go wrong and there'd be nobody around to save me because we were way beyond civilization. We were in a foreign land. At least, it felt that way. And it made my heart pound and stomach churn. But I'd told him I'd do it, so it was too late to back out. We headed for his house, or what used to be. He'd asked this as a favor, and he'd never before asked for one, and so I knew I couldn't refuse. Afterwards, I'd treat him to lunch, anywhere he wanted to go.

As we drove on, I couldn't help thinking it'd been four whole years since the eastern flood wall collapsed, sending a wall of water into his house, two blocks from where the levee broke. We reached Tennessee Street. He asked me to stop. A broken foundation slab caught my eye first before I saw all the empty lots, empty driveways and concrete steps. He pointed to the slab. "I'm gonna build it back," he told me.

"You're gonna build it yourself or have someone build it for you?"

"Myself."

"You know how to build a house, Lennus?"

"Nothing to it," he swaggered. "I already drawn up the plans. Someday, I'm gonna be a architect."

"Really? I didn't know that about you. You'll do fine—you'll do terrific. But you have to go to school first."

He took out a joint.

"You don't have to smoke every minute of the day, do you?"

His eyes fixed on the slab. His facial muscles tensed, and for an instant, I had a sense of the enormity of what he'd lost. The isolation was thick on the spot where we stood as the distant calls of blackbirds pierced the stillness in the lonely terrain. He was fading into his own thoughts, like pot fumes into mist.

"Listen," I nudged him, trying to re-capture what we had. I had the overwhelming feeling that there wasn't time to lose —or to worry about ego, looking stupid, or appearing foolish. A devastated area will do that to you. "I will help you," I said fiercely. "Whatever you need, I will help."

It was the first time I'd seen anything in his eyes that wasn't boredom or disdain. I can't explain why I said it or what I thought I'd do. I got tired of seeing dead boys floating in my head, couldn't stand seeing another, an absolute certainty unless somebody reached out and helped him.

"C'mon," I said. "Let's go have lunch. Where would you like to go?"

❧

*W*e went to Bud Rip's Bar. It'd been a watering hole since 1918. It had a carved mahogany bar and engraved tin ceiling. Two men sat at the bar looking like they came from the hills of West Virginia. One had a cap on backwards and a wiry grey beard. The bartender was fleshy. Her hair was thin, straw-colored. She wore a plunging yellow blouse and was gabbing with another customer: "No frickin' way."

We ordered burgers at the bar. I tried strategizing while we waited for our food to arrive. If he made an effort to attend class and get halfway decent grades, I'd pay his way through college. I probably could afford the University of New Orleans; I'd saved some money. And they might have a school of architecture. I'd look into it. Didn't have to figure everything out right now, take one step at a time. I made him an offer. The bartender brought his Barq's. He lifted it to his lips. "We'll see 'bout that," he told me.

"What's there to see about? All you have to do is make good grades. That shouldn't be hard for you."

"I can't make no promises."

"Just do me this one favor."

He waited for me to go on.

"Will you please think it over? I'll even draw up a contract. You finish high school, I'll pay for college. That's quite a deal, don't you think?"

"What's in it for you?"

"Nothing."

He looked at me. That was when I knew: something wasn't right. He said, "I don't want shit from you." It came out of nowhere. There were things I wanted to say, all of them true, to save him—Lennus—but the timing was wrong or he was or I was because he just shut down. We drove back in silence, the way we'd come. I parked, he got out. I headed for the Café, he to the Center.

And when he crossed the street, we saw Alejandro coming our way. Alejandro had been to the Center for some reason or other, maybe delivering something to Odessa. And as their paths happened to cross, Lennus spit at him. His aim was slightly off. He was aiming for his foot, but it landed a fraction to the right, barely missing him. This time, Alejandro didn't ignore it.

He grabbed Lennus by the shirt, shook him, cursing him. He flipped him to the asphalt and got on top of him. I think he totally lost it. Something in him snapped. And I could sense his rage and was afraid he was going to hurt the boy. He kept holding Lennus by the shirt, their faces so close it looked like their noses touched, and he said something I couldn't hear. They were on the ground for seconds before Alejandro yanked up the boy and, when he was solidly to his feet, held him by the arm and dragged him to the Center.

They disappeared inside.

CHAPTER 17

J hurried over, thinking Alejandro might need some
help. The boy lies. It was part of his nature to
twist everything around, and Alejandro was too much of a
gentleman to adequately defend himself.

I stood outside Alice's door. It was open a tiny crack. And
there they were inside—Alice, Lennus, and Alejandro—and I
could hear their voices. Or rather, Alejandro's voice. The
tone, not what he was saying. He wasn't loud, just serious,
fed up and scathing.

I edged closer, hesitant to make myself known. After all,
this wasn't my affair. I didn't want to get into it unless I
had to.

He went on and on, level-headed, but with a low,
wounded voice, the tone telling all. Every once in a while, I'd
hear the boy's voice, sarcastic, in counterpoint, witheringly
disdainful, ripping Alejandro apart, making a joke of him
with his acid tongue, as he did so eloquently, annihilating
and condescending.

Any second now, I told myself, waiting for the boy to give
me reason, but not quite yet.

And then there was nothing.

Alejandro had finished making his point, and there was nothing more to be said. Then came Alice's voice—probing, subdued, directed at her son. His response dripped with sarcasm, and Alice shot something back. Alejandro raised his voice, and soon all three were speaking at once, until Alice's voice finally reigned. This time I could hear clearly: "What am I gonna do with you? Answer me, Lennus. *What am I gonna do with you?*"

"Why don't you dump me in the river? Throw me in the trash. Ain't that what you want? Get rid of your only son? Now tell the truth, ain't it?"

"You hush your filthy mouth! Your mama didn't raise you to treat people that way. Your daddy'd be disgusted. If he were alive ... why... why..."

Then Lennus said something, and Alice shouted: "*Shut up!*" before breaking down in tears.

No sounds, except for weeping.

The door was slightly ajar. I peeked in, saw Alejandro standing with his chin held high, solemn and respectful, hands behind his back, not looking at Alice. There were creases across his forehead and worry lines around his mouth. His stance reminded me of an Indian, the kind you used to see in front of tobacco shops. That's when I slipped in.

I stood inside the door.

Nobody seemed surprised, like they'd known all along.

Miserably, Alice glanced from me to her boy. "What are we gonna *do* with you?" She sounded pathetic, eyes brimming. "You want to go to the Youth Study Center? Is that what you want, Lennus?"

"What's that?" I whispered to Alejandro.

He said, "Juvenile lockup in Gentilly."

"You treat me with *contempt*," she said. "And I've just about

154

had enough. One day, if you continue, you're gonna end up in prison, with all the uncontrollable boys who grow up to be men who hate everybody, who bring shame upon their families and shame upon themselves. Is that what you want, Lennus?"

She stood leaning over the desk, fists clinched, facing him.

She put the palms of her hands on the desk and stared, infuriated at him, but Lennus wasn't looking. He hid behind his merriment, as if this were some kind of joke.

"Look at me," she snapped. *"And answer your mother—"*

All blissful calm. He stood, hands in pockets, looking as though he could leave whenever he got ready; he just wasn't ready yet.

And then: "Stay cool. Stay calm. Ain't no big deal," he said. "Don't get so fuckin' mad."

"Don't *talk* to me that *way!*" Fist pounding the desk. "You apologize this minute."

"Ain't apologizing to nobody."

Alice had run out of words. She turned helplessly to Alejandro. He stood in the same position, not moving, out of respect for her.

"Will you take him?" she asked.

Alejandro looked her way.

"Will you take my son?" she said. "He doesn't listen to me. I'm useless to him. For the first time in my life—God help me —I give up. Will you *take* him?" She turned to Lennus. "I don't even think he loves me. I think he's stopped loving me."

Lennus blinked.

"There's no one he loves," Alice murmured. "And when you don't have that, when you don't love the one who made you, there's nothing to live for. Will you take my son?"

Alejandro stuttered. "I... no sure what you mean."

"Will you take my son?"

Alice bowed her head. She sat down, biting her lip. Her lids were red. She seemed distraught, defeated. "I just mean...," she mumbled, "look after him please. Don't let him get away with things. I'll pay you what I can. Just keep an eye on him. I know this is terrible, I'm asking you to save him. If I wasn't so... if I wasn't so afraid... please, I'm begging you... If he doesn't have someone put a heavy foot in front of him, he'll end up a monster. He'll end up dead." She began weeping and all of us looked away.

After a moment, she removed her hands from her eyes and drew in her breath. "You have my permission..." She spoke slightly above a whisper, exhaling, but her words were clear. "... to do whatever you want. I know you're a good man. Don't let him get away with things."

Alejandro looked horrified. He turned away and back to her, amazement in his eyes as if he might be imagining it.

She cried out, "*I don't want my child to die—*"

He took that in. It seemed as if he understood the desperation behind the words, the terrified look she gave, and he nodded. He turned to Lennus.

"I have son your age," he said. "Not see him much but see him when I can. He live with his mamá. He not like you."

He spoke matter-of-factly but with depth of feeling. He was about to say something more when Lennus cut him short.

"Some father you are—skip out on your own son."

"I no skip out. No money. He better off in Mexico. One day I be with him."

"Leaving him in spic city. Deadbeat motherfucka—"

The boy's eyes were a wonder: provocative, vicious. He had a hardness I wasn't used to.

"His mamá, she care for him. I send money every month. His tuition and clothes and food—"

"You don't have to explain," Alice's voice broke in. "Can't you see he's goading you?"

"I was about to say..." Alejandro spoke with dignity, turning once more to Lennus. "You try get away with things. This time you have big trouble. Two big trouble: Me and your mamá."

"Three big trouble," I hastened. "I'm in on this with you."

"Your mamá and me and Jamila," Alejandro spoke with growing confidence. "We make big hell for you. If you so much as blink—"

"So much as try to skip school," Alice threatened, "we're coming after you—"

"If you try smoking pot," I added, "we're gonna make your life miserable—"

"If you spit at me again," Alejandro enjoined, "me, your mamá, Jamila—we find a fitting punishment."

"We're gonna nail you to the wall 'til your blood drips," I said, recalling the threat Uncle Asaad used to make, disciplining his seven kids.

"We'll get everybody at the Center to think up things." Alice was resolute. "Your life won't be worth living if you're not polite and respectful. You're not the only one in this world. There are other people hurting. Do you hear me, Lennus?"

"We may not be able to stop you," I said, "but we'll make your life so bad you won't know which way is up."

We were shouting all at once, sweet relief all over our faces, when he'd had just about enough of us. Lennus slammed the door behind him, something he had a great talent for, but it was getting kind of old.

"Good luck," I shouted after him, "on getting rid of us!" And then Alejandro slapped my palm, giving me a high five.

CHAPTER 18

$\mathcal{I}$t was difficult arranging my life between organizing the symposium and helping Blue get the Café started, and I found myself working weekends and evenings to catch up. When I had a moment to reflect, I marveled at how much my life had changed since Blue came on the scene.

Ever since I was old enough to leave home, I protected my privacy and independence, having finally been set free from the sheltered environment my parents provided because they loved me so much. The only problem was, they loved me so much I couldn't breathe. And so, the spoiled brat that I was, I did the opposite of what they wanted, which was for me to marry a Lebanese, the same way Mama did when she was only eighteen. Any time a Lebanese man so much as showed a special interest, I ran the other way. Then one day I woke up and looked in my bedroom mirror, and there staring back at me was a fifty-one-year-old woman who was husbandless and childless.

But it wasn't so bad. I loved my job, my city, and all the times I was fancy-free. Little did I realize that on a Sunday when I was clueless, Blue would re-enter my life, bringing surprises around every corner—crises that had to be put down, busybody relatives, lost boys, and Latino workers flowing in and out of my door—until I was stripped of all my privacy. And to my stunned disbelief and utter amazement, I grudgingly had to admit my life was richer for it.

And then one evening, my landline rang.

"Blue," I called out, "it's for you."

We were back at my house late Tuesday. Blue had prepared *laham mishwi* (shish kabob) and *mjaddarra* (lentils) for supper, and after we'd had our fill, we retreated into the living room to do our favorite thing: a Bud for me, red wine for her.

We'd been talking about the grand opening party coming up on Thursday night. After all our heavy planning and the smaller parties that served as warmups—the dinner party with the ruined seafood; the failed supper with Lennus and Alice; the tea party that went ballistic—the big night was nearly here. Blue got up and came over to take the phone from me.

"Hello," she said, taking my place in the armchair. I went over to the sofa where she had been sitting. She nodded as she listened, not saying a word. And then, "yes... yes..." That was all. And "yes... yes..." she repeated. "And what did he say?" She gasped, closed her eyes, and opened them momentarily; I could see the heartache trapped in them. "When will it be?" More silence. "Rima's coming? When? Who'll be coming with her? I'll get back to you." She hung up.

Blue sat still, as if she couldn't move.

"Blue, what's going on?" She'd been talking with Meredith.

Her head was bent low, hand still holding the receiver. Slowly, she placed it in its cradle and fumbled for her wine. She swallowed a sip and set the glass on a side table. She placed the palms of her hands against her cheeks and leveled her gaze at me. "You know," she said haltingly, "ever since Sally Ann had her gastric bypass surgery, she's been complaining of a lot of pain."

"Yes, Meredith told me."

"And we thought this had something to do with the surgery. Ever since her surgery, she's hardly been able to eat. The only thing she can eat is melon and salty pretzels. Even that she can't keep down."

"I know."

"She's been going to a lot of doctors. No one knew what was wrong. And last week she went to a new one." Blue struggled to keep her voice from wavering. "This new doctor... he did a series of tests."

She blinked at her trembling hand.

"And what did he say?"

"He got the results back... late this afternoon."

"And...?"

"Cancer."

"*Oh my god...*"

"Pancreatic."

She pressed her palms against her cheeks, letting one slide to her throat. It dropped uselessly to her lap. "I have to think," she said fretfully. Both hands went to her ears and then she reached for her glass of wine. She drank till it was empty and got up. "I'll be back." She hurried into the hall; I could hear noises in the kitchen.

When she returned, she sat down, holding her newly-filled glass. "And so," she went on, "they're going to operate Friday. See if it has spread. If it's contained within the pancreas, they'll take it all out. It's going to be a long operation."

"And if not? If it's spread?"

"They'll sew her back up."

"Where will it be?"

"At home."

"Harbortown Memorial?"

"Yes."

"Friday morning?"

"Yes."

We sat once again in silence.

Presently, she picked up the phone. "Honey," she said uncertainly, "do you remember Sally Ann's number?"

I took the receiver from her hand, dialed the number, and handed it to her.

"Hello, hello, Sally Ann?" she said anxiously. "Hello, my love, how are you? I just spoke with Meredith. How do you feel?" Pause. "When is your sister coming?" Pause. "I'll be with you for the operation. But I was wondering if you'd want to do this: Do you feel well enough to come here tomorrow?" Pause. "I was thinking we could pay a visit to a saint's shrine." Pause. "This saint was a local priest. He's known for his miraculous healing. There's a shrine named in his honor. I could call to make the reservation. They'll have witnesses to give testimony." Pause. "These are people who will tell us how the priest interceded on their behalf and cured them of their illnesses. They'll pray with us, give us a tour. I'll come home with you afterwards." Long pause. "Never mind about that... yes... bring them with you. I'll see you tomorrow. Meet me at the Café. Ten. *Ana bahibbik... I love you...*"

She put down the receiver.

The first thing I thought: They were playing some kind of game. A sadistic, demonic one, to get Blue to come home. Meredith and I had been in touch. She, Sally Ann, and Frankie had been to Jeremiah, Mississippi, to load up Blue's heavy furniture to bring back to Harbortown, all without Blue's knowledge. They'd put the furniture in storage, thinking that when Blue did come home, they'd find a place for her to live.

I hadn't told them about her addled memory, hadn't warned them about my fears, some instinct of mine putting it off till, somehow, it never got done, and now a guilt came over me for not preparing them for what they needed to know.

In truth, I didn't know what to do. Should I be on the side of my cousins and let them take Blue home to be nursed and fretted over and coddled 'til she died of boredom? Or be on the side of Blue? To be on the side of Blue meant watching her forgetfulness intensify, witnessing dementia set in, while she had a café/bar to run, dumping on her family's shoulders the heavy burden of financial debt. But to be on the side of Blue meant being on the side of dreams and on the side of Oretha Castle and having confidence in the future and pride in one's high goals.

I wasn't at all convinced that having a business would be all that terrible. I could count on one side of the ledger a dozen reasons for not having it, and on the other, only one: it would be a hell of a grand adventure. *Seize joy*, my soul cried out. Never mind Blue wouldn't be able to run it. Never mind the question of what to do with it.

Across the room, Blue half-whispered, "I remember when her mama went through this." Her head rested against the back of the chair. "You were just a little girl at the time."

"She had cancer too, didn't she?"

I remembered Blue's sister. Aunt Nayla had taken me to Sunday Mass when I was no more than five years old. I'd been staring at the singing choir high up in the loft at the back of the church when she told me to turn around—not harshly, but matter-of-factly. I didn't see her for weeks after that and asked Mama where she was. She told me Aunt

Nayla was in the hospital. I asked if I could visit her, and Mama gave me a straight, honest no.

"Yes," Blue answered. "She had breast cancer, honey. In those days, they didn't have much to ease the pain, and when I visited her in the hospital, I could hear her screaming all the way down the hall."

"Did you wish she would die so she wouldn't have to suffer so?"

"No." Blue's voice faltered. "I never wanted her to leave me."

"What's going on tomorrow?"

"They'll all be coming over."

"Who? Sally Ann?"

"Yes. And Sally Ann's husband and sister and... and... her sister's husband and... her cousin..."

"Frankie and Rima and Ed and Meredith?"

"Yes. They'll all be coming."

Rima was Sally Ann's older sister. She'd married Ed Mansour when she was eighteen and gone to live with him in Dallas. I figured they must be flying into Harbortown from Texas, on Ed's private jet.

"They'll all meet me at the Café," said Blue. "We'll head over to the shrine. I'll call first thing in the morning to schedule it. I thought this might be a way to comfort Sally Ann. And, you know, she didn't put up a fuss. She surprised me—I thought she'd say no. But she *wants* to come. I could hear it in her voice. We'll drive home later in the day. She'll need to check into the hospital on Thursday. I'll go back with her tomorrow."

The realization of what the future held seemed unbearable to Blue, and she grew pale and silent.

"Don't you think this might be some kind of trick?" I asked.

She looked up, bewildered.

"A ploy to get you home? I mean, I don't know, I'm not sure, Blue. But think about it. Why would Sally Ann want to come all this way to visit the shrine of a saint she's never even heard of? And if it's a trick—and I'm not saying for sure —it's brilliant, don't you think? Now they won't have to connive to get you back to Harbortown because you've already agreed to go. You see what I'm saying?"

Blue shot me a look of contempt. "You think they're lying about the cancer? You think they'd do a thing like that? Why, Jamila, what's wrong with you? They may be bossy but never cruel."

"If you're going home with them to Harbortown, will you be coming back for the celebration?"

Blue gave a look of bewilderment, as if she didn't know what I was talking about. Then, suddenly, she seemed to understand. She shook her head in reply, as though she couldn't find her true voice.

"Don't worry, Blue," I sighed. "I'll take care of everything."

"Honey, shouldn't we cancel it?"

"I don't think so. Everything's set. Odessa, Alejandro, and Gaynelle will help."

Gaynelle was the new cook we'd hired to take the place of Nacho.

"I feel terrible leaving you with this."

"Your place is with her. So don't even think about it."

"I love her so much..." Blue's voice wavered. "I could never live with myself if I didn't go be with her."

"Don't worry about the guests. The guests will understand. Don't worry about anything."

"I feel terrible—"

"Don't, please! The only important thing is Sally Ann."

~

*T*hat night, Blue slept in my guest bedroom. She didn't want to go back to the Café. I came to her room late to wish her good night and saw her sitting in the armchair in the corner, lights out, surrounded by evening darkness. It brought back memories from more than twenty years ago—the time after Meredith's twin brother died, when Aunt Marcia was visiting her. Back then, Meredith and her husband, Abe, were living in Des Allemands, Louisiana, where Abe had an ophthalmology practice. The day I went to visit, Aunt Marcia was sitting in Meredith's guest bedroom.

It was September 1986, eighteen days after Michael died. Though it was mid-morning and sunny, the curtains had been drawn. Aunt Marcia, a frail 88-year-old, sat silently in the dark, staring at the bed, arms limp on the chair.

"Aunt Marcia..." I touched her arm. It was soft—icy. I got down on my knees before her.

She clung to me. "Jamila, your mama and daddy loved you. Oh, they loved you so much."

She seemed to want to talk. Or perhaps she knew how much I wanted to hear the family story and sensed the time was right to tell it. Her son, Michael, had died in his sleep of a heart attack. There'd been so many deaths in recent years: her sister who'd lived in Alabama and was *sitty* to the seven A-Baki kids; my daddy; Uncle Imad; her 105-year-old mother; and now her 47-year-old son, Michael.

Contained in her voice, an unmistakable grief. A humility hung over her, and it reminded me of my dad. I pulled up a chair. She began telling me about the "big house," the beautiful Colonial mansion on the beachfront where we grew up. Her family first lived over a dry goods store on 25th Avenue, she told me, and later bought the "big house." Everybody in the family lived there—my mom and dad, her mother, Uncle

Imad and Aunt Nayla, and everybody's children—all except for her.

She'd married and moved to Burlington, North Carolina, with the man she'd recently married. After a few years, they returned to Harbortown and built their own home across from the beachfront highway, two blocks from the "big house." Soon, Uncle Imad was living in his own home, next door to my mom and dad. Sitty Yasmine moved in with Aunt Marcia.

She breathed in, then let it out.

"Honey, don't let them tell you any differently," she said, a smile illuminating her eyes. "*I* was the one introduced Rima to Ed." Joyfully, she began telling the story of the courtship of Ed and Rima. And when she finished, she started on my mom and dad.

"I introduced your mama to your daddy. I was married then and living in North Carolina. I came back to Harbortown for a visit and brought your mama down with me. She was a very young girl then. I remember it was dark when we first arrived in Harbortown and she couldn't see the Mississippi Sound. And when she woke up the next morning and looked out the window, she said, 'Oh, Marcia, how could you have left *this*?' And when your daddy met your mama, he fell head over heels in love. He was crazy about your mama. I think she kind of loved him, too."

Mama was sixteen when she met Daddy, an older man. I thought her saying "she kind of loved him, too" was a bit of an exaggeration. Surely Mama liked Daddy and respected his business sense and the fact that he was Lebanese, which was a big deal in Lebanese families trying to marry off a daughter. But I didn't think at that stage of the game she loved him, though no doubt it came later.

I changed the subject. "How did you meet Uncle Walid?"

Aunt Marcia settled into the story. "I was working in the

store one day. I remember we were very busy. A lot of customers were there who needed tending to. A regional buyer for the store dropped by and Walid was with him. I don't know if he was with him on business or just came along as a friend. But your daddy was very busy and asked if I would entertain them. I said, 'Moawad, is he nice?' Your daddy said, 'Yes, very nice.'"

Her glow reached full measure, recalling those romantic days.

"And so I entertained them and they left," she said. "Later, Walid called me from North Carolina and said he was coming down to take me to the Super Bowl. And do you know, we'd only seen each other twice when he asked me to marry him. He said, 'Marcia, I have to go to New Orleans on business and I want you to think about it and give me your answer when I return.' I said, 'Walid, I don't need to think about it. My answer is yes.' That night, Mama was sleeping. I woke her up. I told her Walid had proposed to me and she was stunned. I was thirty-eight years old when I married Walid. He told me to keep it a secret. The only one I told was Mama. I remember we had a ladies get-together—I was a member of the Eastern Star—and we were playing some sort of game where you'd go around the table and try to guess everybody's secret. A friend's turn came up and she said, 'Marcia, are you engaged?' I said yes. It caused such a commotion. Everybody was thrilled."

Her head moved with excitement, her tone recalling long ago. She must have been thinking she'd talked long enough for she suggested we go into the den. I held her arm for support. Together we plodded into the den to be with Meredith and Abe. Later, when it was time to leave, I came back into the little room where she'd gone to take her nap and bent over her bed. She awakened, eyes startled, and clung to me like a child. She knew I was leaving and thanked me many times for coming, said how much she loved me, over and over again. I kissed her and left.

And now in my guest bedroom, Blue sat in the dark. It felt as if I'd been through this many years before, and so I braced myself for the routine. I touched Blue's mottled arm. "Are you all right?" I could barely see her face.

Her voice cut through the dark.

"This reminds me so much of Nayla. Oh, what happened, darlin'? One day we're all so happy and going about our business and the next day they're all gone." Blue leaned forward and, in the shadows, a wetness shone in her eyes. "Will you come with me tomorrow?"

"Sure. Now you get some sleep, Blue. We've got a busy day tomorrow."

CHAPTER 19

With a little research and investigation, I managed to figure out the name of Blue's saint, who had miraculously healed the sick. He wasn't quite a saint as yet, but well on his way to becoming one.

His name was Francis Xavier Seelos.

And once I got the number of the shrine named in his honor, I called to make a reservation. Over the phone, the woman told me that the perfect time for us to visit would be in the afternoon. And so we made the reservation for half past one. The woman promised there'd be somebody at the Shrine to pray with us, lead us on a tour, and give witness.

That morning, Blue called Sally Ann.

She instructed her to meet us at the Café at eleven o'clock and she'd take us out to brunch prior to our visit to the Francis Seelos Shrine. We were to gather in the courtyard on the grounds of St. Mary's Annunciation Church in the Irish Channel and ring the bell at the back of the church, which happened to be the entrance to the Blessed Seelos Museum. At 1:30 sharp, with all of us gathered behind her, Blue rang the doorbell.

An old man answered the door.

He looked to be in his eighties. He was stocky with hyaline blue eyes and a round, full-fleshed, rosy face. The top of his head was bald, tufts of white hair clinging to the sides. He wore a cotton shirt and baggy pants. He might have been a retired priest or deacon or lay volunteer. He seemed the reticent type and accommodating. But when Blue announced we'd made reservations to tour the Museum, he was not shy in his response. "It's closed," he said.

Blue looked at him in disbelief. "But the lady told us to come this afternoon."

"Who told you?"

Blue looked at me.

"Judy," I said.

"Julie? Julie? But the Museum's closed."

"She said it doesn't close 'til three."

"What time is it?"

"Exactly one thirty," I said sharply. "And these people have come all the way from Mississippi, to be here."

He blinked. "Come in," he said placidly, "I'll give you an abbreviated tour."

The Museum was long and narrow, the floor tiles sparkling clean. Large paintings of Seelos hung from one wall alongside paintings of the Stations of the Cross. Paraphernalia related to the life of Seelos was encased in glass. A life-sized bronze statue of the Redemptorist missionary priest stood across from a door that opened onto the side of the church altar. Two men bent forward, studiously peering into glass cases.

The old man began telling about the life of Francis Seelos, speaking from rote memory, the intensity of his concentration signaling he was having trouble remembering facts, the pupils of his eyes rolling back in his head as he valiantly struggled to recall.

Seelos was born in 1819, he told us, in Füssen, Germany, one of twelve siblings. He died in 1867 of yellow fever in New Orleans.

"Where *was* I?" he repeated, and Ed had to remind him where he'd left off.

He said Seelos became pastor of Sts. Peter and Paul Church in Cumberland, Maryland, and later transferred to a parish ministry in Annapolis, and that in 1863, during the time of the Civil War, Seelos worried that the Redemptorist seminarians might be drafted into battle. At that point, Seelos met with Abraham Lincoln to beg him not to send them to the front line. But when Lincoln informed Seelos that only ordained priests could be excused from battle, Seelos rushed to visit the bishop to see what could be done. And that's when the old man's recitation came to an abrupt halt. Utterly bewildered, he turned to his two guests.

"Pardon me... excuse me, archbishop. Am I explaining it right?" the old man wanted to know. "Was it the bishop or archbishop that Seelos went to see?" He turned to us. "This" —he nodded in their direction—"is the archbishop from Baltimore and this gentleman is a priest from Baltimore."

"Nice to meet you, archbishop." Ed stepped forward. "Nice to meet you, Father. My name's Ed. And this is—"

"*No,*" the priest cut him off, "you've got it wrong. *He's* the archbishop and *I'm* the priest. Nice to meet you, Fred."

The archbishop turned to the old man. "Seelos first approached the bishop and then the archbishop to see what could be done about getting the seminarians exempt from fighting. They came up with a plan to ordain them at once. And that seemed to solve the problem."

The old man looked pleased.

He gathered himself up, preparing to continue his recitation, but I could tell by the change of expression and worry in his eyes that he seemed to have lost confidence in the viability of his working memory. He began rattling off other facts, not in any particular order but jumping from one to the other, randomly, disjointedly, in confusion about the life of Seelos, switching from one period of his life to another. Ultimately, he came to the part about the final days of Seelos, telling the story of when Mother Mary came to him.

"It was October 2nd," he related. "Father Seelos was on his deathbed, dying of yellow fever, when his friend, Brother Kenning, came to visit. Father Seelos told his old friend he'd just seen the Virgin Mother."

"'How many times has she appeared to you?' Brother Kenning asked.

"'Twice,' Father Seelos whispered.

"'Was she beautiful?' asked Brother Kenning.

"'Oh, how beautiful is the Mother of God.'

"And then Father Seelos looked at Brother Kenning as if he had so much more to tell him but was too weak to go on," the old man related. "And two days later, Father Seelos was dead."

"*For the love of Jesus!*" Blue emoted.

"Are you all right?" Frankie moved toward her.

"Yes..."

"You look like you've seen a ghost."

"No... no... I'm fine," Blue murmured. "It took me by surprise, is all."

Meredith's eyes narrowed. "What took you by surprise?"

You could see in Blue's face her longing to reveal all, but she bit her lip, wrung her hands and stood pensively before them. And when she no longer could contain herself, these words came tumbling out: "It's just that I felt so *alone*..." No longer holding back, her words exploded on all of us. "You see," Blue said breathlessly, "Mother Mary came to *me*."

In the stillness, everybody glared at her, even the archbishop, as if some wicked naked body part lay exposed upon a gurney.

Meredith shook her head.

"Oh, let me guess," she said dramatically, "where this fantastic meeting might have occurred. Was she looking up from some pothole on Oretha Castle Haley? Or peering through the broken glass from that burnt-out shell of a school building?"

"Oh, hush up! That's enough!"

"Yes, yes... we want to know..." Meredith could not restrain herself. "Would you please tell us *where?*"

"You're being so disrespectful..."

"Don't leave us in suspense," Meredith said, piling it on. "It's not often Mother Mary descends from heaven to pay a visit to us mortals. As, of course, she did with you. Come on, Blue, we're all ears. Don't make us get down on our knees and beg."

"*Stop it right now.*" Blue hoisted herself up.

By now, she fully recognized the enormity of her error. Ed squeezed Rima's hand. The archbishop and priest seemed fascinated. The old man gazed curiously, craning his neck. This time Blue was steaming mad. She was about to unload on Meredith when she inexplicably had a change of heart.

She lowered her voice, seeming to take control of her emotions.

"You're making a scene, darlin'," she said. "And making me feel ashamed. Besides, you've interrupted this nice gentleman." Blue turned to her host. "I'd like to *apologize,*" she said to the old man. "I know your time is valuable. Please—go on."

"Are we all through here?" he intoned.

Blue looked stunned, her eyes a deeper shade of blue than his. The "tour," barely begun, was over.

"How close is Seelos to getting canonized?" I blurted out,

looking at the archbishop. I knew the old man wouldn't know.

"I don't know."

"Doesn't he need one more miracle to be canonized a saint?"

"He had that five years ago," the archbishop said blandly.

"I didn't know that..." I stammered, trying my best to keep us here awhile, struggling mindlessly to help Blue. "Who was the beneficiary of the miracle?"

"A woman from Annapolis," the archbishop said. "Her esophageal cancer had spread to her liver, lungs, and back, and she wasn't expected to live."

Meredith, unable to hide her disdain, ranted in Sally Ann's ear, while Sally Ann tried her best to listen. But at the mere mention of "cancer," Sally Ann leaned forward, straining to catch whatever Seelos had done to save the woman.

"It was five years ago?" I persisted.

"Eight." The archbishop seemed unsure.

"And where are we now in the process?"

"I don't know," he said indifferently. "All the miracles have been recorded and the paperwork sent to the Vatican's Congregation of the Causes of the Saints. And now it's up to the Holy Father."

We waited, I don't know why. I don't know what we were expecting to hear. We waited and waited, and, finally, the old man came to life.

"Ready to go?" he said.

We followed him out of the Museum onto the grounds of the church, Meredith scurrying after Blue, trying her best to provoke a fight. But Blue was too smart for her. She trotted a little ahead, hustling to reach the archbishop, coolly beseeching him, "Can you tell us about the miracles?"

"I've witnessed a miracle." The old man, walking ahead, turned back to look at Blue.

"You have?" Blue asked eagerly.

"I had open-heart surgery and was ripped open."

"Yes?"

"It's a complicated story." The old man mumbled something about having had a stent put in and called out to the archbishop. "You know what that is, don't you?"

"I sure do," replied the archbishop.

"And... and..." Blue entreated, "so what was the miracle?"

Meredith couldn't resist. "I want to hear about the *real* miracle: the day you talked to the Virgin Mary."

"Will you *please stop it?*" Blue halted. "I never said I *talked* to Her. I only said She came to me. If you will please hold your horses, I'll tell you all about it over drinks at the Café. And in the car driving home, you can ask whatever you like, if that's all right with you." Cheeks flushed, Blue quickly turned to the old man. "You were telling us about the miracle?"

The old man's eyes shone. "Seelos took my hand. And there was a woman who'd come to the Shrine, and she was walking where we are now, and she fell and Seelos helped her up. She saw him."

"And there were some children," the archbishop joined in, his expression quite animated, "and they were..." but I couldn't catch the rest of it; he was walking too far ahead. The only thing I caught was something about Seelos holding their hands.

We followed them into the gift shop. Ed offered a donation.

"Give it to the gift-shop ladies," the old man advised.

He hadn't even introduced himself. But then he must have had a tinge of conscience because he said something about us having had an "abbreviated" tour and that someday we should come back. We left, heading for the Café. The plan was for Blue to pick up her bags and ride back with them to Harbortown.

It was nearly three o'clock.

It was a beautiful, hyaline day, a pale blue sky above.

As we approached Oretha Castle, I saw the steel girders of the elevated Pontchartrain Expressway and beyond it, rising above it, the gilded dome of St. John the Baptist Church. I was hoping Ed and Rima might see the street in its better light. But as we drove under the expressway, they were all there together: derelicts sleeping under the expressway or sitting shoulder to shoulder on the sidewalk along the great stretch of Boulevard, their ripped blankets and grimy sheets piled like hillocks beside them, smoking cigarettes, listening to radios, standing on the corner eating from paper plates.

And beyond that, for all the world to see, row upon row of For Sale signs on dingy buildings, and the blackened, burnt-out roof of the abandoned school building, with Ed and Rima, wide-eyed, rubbernecking.

I was embarrassed and ashamed.

They lived in Dallas, in a gorgeous home in a gated community, reaping the rewards of a life of work. Not only did Ed work long hours at his business, but he was also a city council member, giving back to his community. And he worked tirelessly raising funds for St. Jude's Children's Hospital. He was a hero in my eyes. And here he was on this hard-luck street. What had I been thinking, trying to show it in its better light? There was no better light.

And then it dawned on me: Maybe that was the point.

For if there was such a thing as the Blessed Mother giving Blue a sign of where to go for whatever She needed her to do, surely She wouldn't have pointed her to a clean, well-managed street.

If this entire episode in Blue's life was really what she

thought it was, some fling at human kindness, surely she'd be directed to go where she could do some good. And where else but in this lost, dying, rodent-infested, heartbreak of a dreamless ghetto—for wasn't that the point?

That is, if the "voice" had actually spoken.

I honestly wasn't sure.

I didn't know what to believe, whether to believe Blue and what she believed, or what my rational mind told me. I knew if I were to believe in the latter, I couldn't believe in Blue. I couldn't believe in any of this: this Boulevard, our lives, the possibilities for the future. And so there was no hiding.

We stopped and parked the car. We got out and followed the sidewalk to the entrance to the Café. We were heading toward the porch when we saw something blocking the doorway: A human lump stretched across the threshold.

Sally Ann and Meredith saw it first. During their entire visit, Sally Ann and Meredith had been visibly shaken, each carrying a heavy load. The moment I saw their stricken faces, I knew I'd been wrong about them. Sally Ann not only looked emaciated, but she also seemed too physically weak to carry on, having faded in the last few hours.

Something terrible was happening to her. And they weren't coping with it very well. They'd known each other since they were babies, seeing each other nearly every day, calling several times a day. Sally Ann was Meredith's alter ego, her inseparable, devoted friend and cousin. And everyone knew there was no light at the end of this tunnel, not with this disease.

Sally Ann had been in chronic pain, Meredith told me over brunch. And Meredith had been with her every step of the way, through the vomiting and weakness, the repeated trips to the hospital, each dealing with her own grief, going through their own hell. But when they saw this "thing" ahead, they went on high alert.

Sally Ann gasped. Ed and Frankie stood frozen before reaching the steps, but Sally Ann and Meredith did not break their stride. They ascended the steps, reached the porch, and looked down upon the human lump.

An old man.

A cap, with the logo "Atlantic Company," could not conceal his silver hair. He wore a white, striped shirt, loose jeans, and tennis shoes. His face contained dark shadows, high cheekbones, and a slender nose that fanned out into the wider nostrils. His arms were long and slender, hands long, oddly poignant in their gaunt gracefulness. An empty bottle of Thunderbird lay beside him.

"Help me up," he beckoned Meredith.

"Fuck you," she said right back.

"Hey, you gotta couple bucks for a cup 'a coffee?"

"Get up. Or I'm calling the cops."

Everything about him was old except for his graceful hands. Defiance shone in his eyes, a wicked flashing humor. He scowled and stumbled to his feet while Ed and Frankie glared from the sidewalk. We watched as he gained balance, and, when he stood solidly on his feet, he stumbled past my cousins and tread shakily down the steps. He walked past all of us, reeking of booze. He turned once and slid the back of his hand lazily across his mouth. The wicked grin re-emerged. He looked Meredith and Sally Ann up and down. They stared petulantly back.

"Hey, if I looked like you two gals," he grinned, "I'd throw myself in front of a bus."

He strutted away, then turned, appraising us a final time.

"Hell, if I looked like you," he added, "I'd drown myself in the river."

Sally Ann stepped forward, not to be outdone. "And if I had your life, asshole, I'd *incinerate* myself."

"Shut up, Sally Ann!" Frankie protested.

"*I will not.*" Her hands dug into her shrunken hips. "You think you can hurt my feelings? Please allow me to enlighten you. I've heard a lot worse insults from better people than you. You keep your drunken self off our porch."

She did not take her eyes off him as he sneered and staggered away, making his way toward Downtown.

CHAPTER 20

"*J*'ve been over it a thousand times."

We were in the front room of the Café, sitting at tables near the bar. Blue poured herself some wine, but nobody else wanted anything. The tableau reminded me of Meredith's dad's "criminal court" sessions after his twins had misbehaved.

When Meredith and Michael were in junior high, Uncle Walid would hold mock family court around Aunt Marcia's pinewood dining table whenever the twins got in trouble. He'd hear their version of events before imposing a sentence upon the guilty. It was all in good fun, sometimes hilarious to watch, never meant to be taken seriously. But in this particular circumstance, no one was in a laughing mood.

"I've been over it a thousand times," Blue repeated.

Frankie and Ed had been reading her the riot act. They insisted she close her Café doors and leave the premises at once. They were going over the list of dangers: drunks likely to assault her, the homeless searching for a place to squat, not to mention burglars, robbers, perverts, murderers. And if she were lucky enough to escape all that, the painful truth of the matter was that she was throwing away her money, squandering her inheritance.

"It's the *perception....*," Ed kept emphasizing, "the perception this street is crime-ridden. I don't have to live here to know. It reeks of poverty and crime. No one wants to put themselves in danger over a bite to eat or some liquor at the bar, not the right kind of folks. You know that, Blue. I don't have to tell you. It would mean massive financial failure to open up a business on this particular street, especially in today's economy."

"What he's telling you is the *truth,*" Frankie went along. "Even if none of the worst happens and you open and run the business, it'll only be a matter of time before you'll be forced to liquidate. People won't drive to a blighted area. That's not rocket science, just common sense. You'll have your operating expenses to pay with no money coming in. You don't know what it's like going day to day without customers. It's soul-killing. Nothing good will come of this. Get out before you lose your shirt—"

That's when Meredith demanded to know what the hell Blue meant, all this mumbo jumbo about the Virgin Mary. And that unleashed another round of vitriol.

"Why in heaven's name would the Virgin Mary be talking to *you?*"

And that led Blue to exclaim, "I've been over it a thousand times."

"What have you been over?"

"What She said to me that night: '*Go to New Orleans. Make a gathering place. Be there to welcome them for me.*'"

"What did She look like?" Meredith couldn't resist asking.

"I never saw Her. It was a voice."

"What did it sound like?"

"It was loving. Not of this world. It was pure. And it was holy."

"What makes you think it was the Blessed Mother?"

"I just know."

"Have you heard it recently?"

"No. Not since Jeremiah. She spoke to me three nights in a row."

"Maybe that's telling you something," Sally Ann joined in.

"Telling me what?"

"You said you heard it in Jeremiah," Sally Ann pondered, "and that you never heard it after that. Maybe it was a delusion... something emotional going on with you those nights... it never was—what you thought." Sally Ann's skin had turned jaundiced. Her voice had lost its power. From the spirited woman I'd known all my life, she'd degenerated into the shrunken image of the gravely, irreversibly ill.

I'd always thought of her as free-spirited, the princess of our three families, spoiled rotten like the rest of us, only more so than the rest of us. Blue did everything in the world for her; Meredith and I often joked about it. Years ago, Meredith told me, Sally Ann had asked Blue to do something complicated to a long gown she was planning to wear to the Reveler's Ball. Blue labored over her sewing machine for weeks, working on that gown, remaking it to Sally Ann's specifications. When the time came to pick up the gown, Sally Ann brought Meredith along for moral support, thinking Blue was going to give her "some song and dance." When they arrived, Blue began griping about how she'd toiled for hundreds of hours over that gown and Sally Ann, steadfastly holding her own, chirped, "What do you want me to say? *Thank you, thank you, thank you?*"

Another time, Sally Ann informed Blue that she would be hosting Thanksgiving at her house that year and proceeded to give her a list of seven dishes to prepare. Meredith and I joked that when it came our turn to die, we wanted to come back as Sally Ann.

Now, her dull eyes gazed unsteadily.

Skepticism blazed in Meredith's.

"And even if it were *real*...," Meredith insisted, "even if the *impossible* did occur and the Virgin Mary did speak to you, Lord knows she'd never direct you to a hellhole like this. This street's straight out of a horror opera. Besides, I've never known anyone to hear Mary's voice. Have you?"

"Yes." Blue didn't miss a beat.

"Who?"

Blue looked confused, a look I'd seen before. She twitched and bit her lip, and then an alertness came over her. Getting up, not bothering to speak or explain herself, she moved swiftly toward the staircase and hastily ascended the stairs. She did not hold on to the banisters, leaving us watching in the front room, as she disappeared upstairs. Momentarily, she returned. She was holding a book.

"Bernadette," she said, leafing through the pages after returning to where she'd sat before. She turned the pages in search of something, ignoring us while she concentrated, and then a smile lit up her eyes.

"Bernadette Soubirous," she said. "She heard Mary's voice, too. She was a young girl. She saw a beautiful lady, as she called it, at the grotto where she was gathering firewood."

Blue flipped through the pages. "The grotto was at Massabielle," she read, "outside of Lourdes. It was there she claimed to see the first of eighteen visions. At one of them—the thirteenth—she told her family that the beautiful lady said, 'Go to the priests and tell them that a chapel is to be built here. Let processions come hither.'"

Blue held tightly to the book, as if precious words were contained inside. She looked carefully at each of us, her fingertip pressing against one of the paragraphs.

Frankie rolled his eyes.

"Don't you see," he said, grimacing, "how similar that is to what you thought you heard? There's no question you imagined it, forgetting you read about Bernadette and believing it happened to you. Only, forgetting the exact words, you put your own spin on everything, changing it to something familiar: Instead of Lourdes, you made it New Orleans. Instead of a chapel, you made it a bar—a café—"

"You may have something there."

Until then, Rima hadn't said a word. Clearly devastated by her baby sister's illness, she wasn't exactly in a talking mood. I'd always been told Rima's mother had been beautiful, but I never remembered it being so. And yet, clearly, there was no mistaking the physical beauty of her daughter, Rima. When she was seventeen and newly engaged to Ed, I remembered Rima sitting at her mother's table, with Ed by her side, deeply in love, her head resting on his shoulder. I'd looked at her at that moment and couldn't take my eyes off her. She was a young Elizabeth Taylor, only more stunning, it seemed to me, with long, shimmering black hair and deep-brown, sensitive eyes. There was a radiance about Rima. It made an impression on a young girl.

She's over seventy now, I told myself. But still gorgeous and with that sweet nature. Rima mused, trying her best to figure it out.

"It could be," she ventured thoughtfully, "you read it, and as time passed, it seemed to belong to you. People are complicated. Maybe you needed to hear it. There's something about the human psyche we'll never understand."

Everybody waited. Blue took that in. She was seated between Rima and Ed. Frankie looked critically at her from across the table. Meredith, Sally Ann, and I sat at an adjoining table. Blue searched the eyes of all of us.

"No," she said quietly.

She got up, made her way to the bar. She put the book down on the countertop and filled her empty glass from a bottle. She spoke with equanimity as she looked at Rima. "Because I hadn't read about the young girl 'til *after* I heard the voice."

She sipped her wine and went on: "Nothing like this ever happened to me before." She was sitting on a stool, facing us. "I needed to read about those to whom it had. So I checked out this book from the library. There were some similarities between me and the girl. Oh, I know there were differences. The young girl"—she stopped, glancing at the open page— "lived in the South of France. I lived... in Mississippi. Her family was poor. Mine, well-to-do. It was"—she stared at the open page—"1858 when it happened to her, compared with —" She turned blank, her fretful eyes latching onto me.

"2009...," I said hastily, "compared with 2009 with you."

Encouraged, she didn't hesitate. "And last but not least"— she looked sternly at the page again—"this child was 14. I'll be..."

A battle raged in her head. Her desperate efforts to concentrate fell prey to her stolen memory.

"82," I said softly. "Blue, you'll be 82 tomorrow..."

Someone gasped. Blue took a swallow of her wine. Frankie glanced meaningfully at Sally Ann, and Sally Ann squeezed Meredith's hand.

"But there were things I took comfort in," she rallied, forging on as if possessed. "Funny thing, no one believed her either. Some said she was mentally ill. Others thought she was a fraud. The parish priest"—she looked down, reading— "didn't much believe in visions. He told her to prove herself." Blue stepped down from the stool and meandered about the room. She continued reading from the book as if delivering a fascinating story. "He wanted a miracle performed, make the rose bush near where she appeared to Bernadette bud and flower on a certain date. I don't think much came of that."

"But other miracles did occur." Blue had managed to hit

her stride. She stopped pacing and stood with head held high, eager to get her point across. "I won't bother you with the details. The thing that's most important... the thing I want you to know..."—head bent, eyes shining—"is this: I told you that at the thirteenth vision the beautiful lady told Bernadette to tell the priest a chapel was to be built at the site of her visions. And that processions would come. Well, her request to the priest later brought about the creation of the Sanctuary of Our Lady of Lourdes. Believers come from all over the world. Five million pilgrims visit Lourdes each year."

Blue looked up, her face radiant. Triumphantly, she closed the book. Relief flooded over her, the happiest I'd seen in years. Her lips were slightly parted and her blue eyes incandescent.

Dumb eyes stared back.

Meredith was the first to speak.

"Do you honestly *believe* that what *you've* done in this disaster of a rundown 'hood will cause something like that to happen? 'Cause if you do, Blue, if you *do*... that utterly leaves me speechless. You're flat out of your living mind!"

Blue jerked back as if slapped. She looked around, bewildered.

"No no...," Blue countered. "I... I haven't the vaguest idea what will come of this—honestly, I don't..."

She spoke with failing courage and seemed to withdraw within herself. Her lids closed, then slowly opened. She must have seen us gawking and felt the weight of all our doubts. It was like we were watching the carryings-on of some dramatic stage actress, lost in rapt attention, all of us her captive audience, staring at the lone freak—the star.

"You think I'm... grandiose..." Blue stammered, "like I'm trying to convince you of something? All I'm trying to do is *defend* myself against these... *attacks*. Oh my goodness..." she whispered, "all this *attention*. It's Sally Ann we should be thinking of. It's her life that's important." Her words met with more scrutiny and seemed to deepen her humiliation. "... I... I... all I want to do... is... the *right thing*—"

"When will you know it's done?" Meredith snapped.

"I don't know."

"And what will happen after you've done it?"

"I don't know."

"Well then, there's nothing more to be said." Meredith reached for her purse, pulled out a cigarette, and lit it. She stood up and left the room.

"Then I can go *home*," Blue cried out.

"What?" Sally Ann murmured.

"Go home!"

Blue struggled to her feet and took a stumbling step toward Sally Ann, tears forming in her eyes, "be with you *for good!* That's what will happen..."

Sally Ann looked back, and it was a look that said everything, and everybody saw it and knew what it meant, and Blue knew, and the blood drained from her. And then Ed spoke. It was his calm demeanor honed from years of public speaking that made it believable and even possible. "I'll make a deal with you," he said, as if speaking to a child. "I'll agree to buy this place if you will promise to come home permanently."

Just then, the doorbell rang. A timid tap followed.

Blue paused, wiping her eyes. She moved self-consciously toward the door, but Meredith had gotten there first. Standing in the doorway were May and Johnny.

May practically bounced into the room, hugging everyone cheerfully, clasping Sally Ann's hands and enfolding her. Johnny, May's son-in-law, chatted up the men. They apologized for turning down our invitation to meet us at the Shrine (Johnny had been temporarily detained at the office), but wanted to rush over as soon as they could before everybody left for Harbortown. Ed and Rima, wearing their brightest smiles, genuinely pleased to see them, were soon catching up on old times.

The doorbell rang again.

Russell Kalify stood in the doorway. The old bandleader looked dapper, smelling of Clubman cologne. He knew everyone from the old days back when they'd danced to his music at the Broadwater Beach Hotel. He was thrilled at the sight of May, his old eyes taking her in. And as they hugged and kissed each other, I thought about the two of them, how May's husband had died of complications from Alzheimer's years ago and how May was practically Russell's age. He seemed ecstatic in her presence, a reunion with an old friend.

As I looked around the chattering room, I saw Blue standing alone. Her back was to the kitchen, wringing her hands.

"I just stopped over," Russell called out, "to see if everything was all right."

Everybody looked at him.

"Everything's fine," Blue hastened.

"Because I was worried about you, you know." He turned to Ed. "It nearly ended up a tragedy."

Ed squinted.

Russell turned back to Blue. "You didn't tell him?"

"Let's go sit down." Blue rushed us to the tables. "Darlin', what can I get for you?" Blue took May's drink order and headed for the bar. She no sooner began mixing the drink when she stage-whispered for me to come over. She asked me to get everybody's drink orders, but I already knew them by heart: a Manhattan for Russell, vodka tonic for Johnny. I handed them their drinks as Blue put on her best party voice. Ed sat next to Blue at the bar. During a lull in the conversation, he turned to Russell.

"So what was going on?"

The old band leader looked confused.

"The other day," Ed coached, "that nearly ended in a tragedy."

Russell glanced at Blue. "Do you want to tell him?"

Blue looked away.

Ed looked at me. "Do you know?"

I shook my head.

Ed smiled. "Does anyone want to tell me?"

"I didn't mean to say anything I shouldn't have," Russell said contritely. "I'm sorry if I was indiscreet."

He glanced ruefully at Blue, who'd long ago zoned out, pretending she wasn't there, willing herself invisible. Russell mulled over the situation and seemed to come to a conclusion. "I think you should know," he said to Ed, "what's going on 'round here. Some copper thieves were stealing pipe from under the building the other day. The cops caught 'em. But not before they ran through this room and mowed down some ol' ladies—nearly crippling one ol' gal."

"Mowed down—you mean *shot* them?" Johnny looked horrified.

"No... ran over em trying to escape out back."

"God-Almighty!" Johnny turned to Blue. "What are the chances of your moving out right now? It would be foolish to stay another day."

Blue seemed to shrink before our very eyes.

"That homeless guy," Johnny muttered, "at the door the other night. I stayed up all night worrying he'd come back and slit your throat. Then I'd have to order a black wreath for the front door and a stand of roses for the funeral."

"*Holy shit!*" said Frankie, glancing at Blue. "Nothing but fresh game during hunting season."

Blue seemed practically immobilized. I couldn't stand seeing her trapped that way.

"*Stop it,*" I blurted out. "*You're picking on her.* She has plans to get an alarm. She just hasn't got it yet. But she will. And she has a *dog*—"

"A dog?" Meredith hooted. "She falls down the stairs, a *dog's* gonna pick her up? Besides, the old girl's lost her marbles. What possible good would a *dog* do? Unless she's planning on letting the *dog* mix the drinks, cook and serve the food—"

"*LEAVE HER A-LONE...*" It was as if the words came flying out of me. "*... SHE KNOWS WHAT SHE'S DOING—*"

"Blue," Meredith said, "I want you *examined!*"

Blue turned her way.

"Your *head*. You're acting like you're hallucinating. Believing the Blessed Mother spoke to you. Starting a bar in a fucking deserted part of town. After we get Sally Ann taken care of, we're gonna take you to Chester Watson. He's been certified with the American Board of Psychiatry and Neurology in geriatric psychiatry since '95."

Fear ran through Blue. And that's when she leaped up. Hands shaking, chest heaving, sloshing her wine all over the place, she said, "Sally Ann's going to have *surgery*. We should all be thinking of *her!*"

"We're putting out one fire at a time," Frankie said under his breath.

Ed got up. He put down his glass. He seemed resolute, as if he'd come to some decision. "We're just worried about you, that's all. For our peace of mind, let me buy this place."

Ed certainly had the means. He was the son of a man who came to this country from a Lebanese village at the age of 16 and started a small business. Over the years, that business grew to be the world's largest manufacturer of men's pants. And now Ed was at the head of it.

"What would you do with it?" Blue asked.

"That's something I'd have to think about."

Johnny stood up. "I'll buy it. We can always use it for something."

It'd be no sweat off his back either. Johnny Chamoun, along with his father, had owned a chain of movie theaters before branching out into banking. He was a philanthropist in addition to that, having donated over $5 million to build a high-tech theater in the World War II Museum.

Blue turned from him to Ed. "Stop it—you stop all this fuss! This is embarrassing and I won't have it."

She began moving about in agitation. Tears brimmed in her eyes as they fixed darkly on Ed. "What do you think I am —a *majdoob*? Do you think I'm such a fool I didn't know what I was buying? Or that I'm just too old? Am not responsible for what I do? I may have lost some memory, but old folks do from time to time. I know exactly what I did. And I know what I heard. And I know I can handle this. I'll never in a million years be able to convince you, so I want you to leave right now.

"Sally Ann," she said, turning, "I can't come home with you today, baby. If I did, God help me, I would never finish what I have to do. But I love you with all my heart, and I'm coming after the operation. So help me God, I will. May the angels surround you and comfort you and watch over you—"

She was crying so hard. I came to her, put my arms around her. Sally Ann was crying, too, bending over with hands to her face, as if her heart would break. And then everyone got up. Rima helped Sally Ann up and Meredith followed behind them, walking past Blue out the door. The others, heads bent, made their way wretchedly into the street. The exodus seemed to take place in seconds and then Blue and I were alone.

∾

*S*he kept crying as if she couldn't stop. I helped her to her room and stayed with her as she lay in bed. The light faded, and not long after, the room fell into darkness. We stayed that way throughout the evening, me in the chair, Blue lying motionless in bed.

I got up, warmed some soup, but Blue wouldn't eat. I waited 'til Blue was sleeping and walked out onto the gallery. A blood-red moon hung high, beyond the Frederick Douglass Center. A hush had fallen over the street and there wasn't a living soul around. I thought they must have gathered under the overpass to sleep, the homeless, secure in their own companionship, as Blue and I were in this building. I would have to get up before dawn and go to my place and get dressed to go to work. I was way behind in my work. I'd missed a full day of preparations, and the symposium was scheduled to take place in less than a week.

I looked down at the Boulevard and tried to imagine what it had been like so many years ago. I tried to imagine someone stepping off the sidewalk to walk fast into the street, tried to imagine what they were going to and what they were coming from. But my mind wouldn't focus. A failure of imagination. As hard as I tried, I couldn't fathom what had been in those tall buildings so many years ago, what went on with those merchants, what they talked about with their customers, the fun they had, the work they did, what they thought and what they dreamed.

It must have been beautiful and now it is gone.

Death.

That was all I could see and smell on Oretha Castle Haley Boulevard—looking back at me, seeping into my nostrils, spilling down my throat 'til I would soon join them. The end of the world around us, the shuttered decrepitude, the plywood-smothered windows sealing in the memories, a corpse without a funeral. An everlasting and eternal sleep.

CHAPTER 21

*D*eath was all I could think about, and I thought about my family: Mama and Daddy; Uncle Imad; Aunt Nayla; Aunt Marcia; my beloved cousin, Omar, the eldest brother of the seven A-Baki kids; Meredith's twin brother, Michael.

I thought about Meredith when her husband, Abe, got sick. She'd spent the night with me at my house. Abe slept at Ochsner Hospital while Meredith lay inconsolable on my crushed blue velvet sofa.

"I don't think I can stand it," Meredith lamented in the months before her husband died.

It was late July 1990. A little more than three months later, Abe would be dead. I'd recently bought my house.

"You have to," I told her.

"What if this keeps happening? Things keep breaking down?"

"It's just a temporary setback." I'd settled in my armchair, folding my legs under me. "Abe said himself he thought they were broken a while back. This isn't something new. And the radiation will take care of it. That and the brace. Then he can get back on his regular schedule. He can start coming for the chemotherapy every so often like he did before."

"Meanwhile, we come every day for two weeks for his radiation." Meredith gave a heavy sigh. "Melanie's got to register for St. Alphonsus School on August 8th."

"Jeez, that doesn't give you much time."

"This week and next. Wonder if we can't sell the house?" She was still living in Des Allemands, Louisiana, at the time. When Abe found out he had cancer, he sold his medical practice and put his house up for sale. They were planning to move to Harbortown to live with Aunt Marcia. I assumed Abe was setting Meredith up in her mama's house so she wouldn't be alone after he died.

"You'll be able to sell it," I reassured her.

"Des Allemands's dead. Nobody will want our house."

"What about that new doctor who's taking over Abe's practice?"

"I'll ask him. But if he doesn't want it, there's nobody else. We'll have to leave it empty and let the real estate agent handle it."

"Don't worry about the house. Take each day as it comes."

Through the window, a light shone from my neighbor's house. I longed to go to sleep so I could wake up early the next morning to take Meredith to Ochsner. I was sleepy, but I knew she needed to talk. I went to the kitchen, poured cashews into a bowl, fixed a vodka and orange juice for her, and a beer for myself. Returning to the living room, I saw her stretched out on the sofa, head resting on a pillow. She lifted herself, reached for the vodka.

"Melanie hates to leave Des Allemands," she said, taking a sip of her drink. "This is her senior year of high school."

"She'll love Harbortown."

"And Abe, I'm worried about him."

"He doesn't want to leave either?"

"It's not that. His practice is gone. His mother's dead. There's nothing left for him in Des Allemands. It's just that" —Meredith's tone softened; she set down her glass—"he hates moving to Harbortown... like *this.*"

"Sick and all?" I propped my feet on the ottoman. "It's the best thing, you know. You're doing the best thing. Besides, it's better for you this way. Harbortown's closer to New Orleans. When you bring him to Ochsner, you won't have as long a trip."

"I wish we didn't have to come at all."

"You're lucky to have Ochsner. And you're welcome to stay with me."

"It's just... I've got so much to do." She brought the glass to her lips again. There were dark bags under her eyes. "I've got to get the roof fixed on Mama's house. Put in a brand-new kitchen. Glass in the front porch and make the back porch a utility area so I'll have some place to put my washer-dryer. And get rid of those heavy curtains."

"Take one thing at a time. Don't even think about what you've got to do in your mama's house 'til you've moved out of Des Allemands."

"Our furniture's so heavy. They make you pay by the pound. It'll cost five or six thousand dollars."

"Pay it, Meredith. This is a one-time deal. You're never gonna move again."

"And we can't move anything into Mama's house 'til she gets rid of all her furniture."

"Did you tell her?"

"A dozen times."

"Well, tell her again."

"I can't keep telling her..." She said "her" with deep tenderness. She took a cigarette from her purse, lit it, and placed the match in a crystal ashtray. She took several drags.

"How am I going to be *everywhere?*" She flicked the ashes

into the tray, but some fell on the table. She took a napkin, wiped them off. "I've got to be there when they're fixing the roof. I can't leave Mama alone with those men. And I can't leave Abe by himself. And what about the kids? I can't let two teenagers run wild in the streets. I've got to get Edmund ready for college—"

"Will you take one thing at a time? You're gonna go crazy, Meredith. You don't do anything to your mama's house 'til you've moved out of Des Allemands. And you move out of Des Allemands as soon as your mama gets rid of the furniture. As for Edmund, he's a big boy. He can pack his own things."

"Abe can't do any lifting."

"Let the *movers* pack everything. Take him to Sally Ann's. So he won't be tempted to pick up anything."

"He can't stay there. All those children running round." Miserably, she took another drag. Smoke streamed from her nostrils as she smashed the cigarette in the tray. "How long a ride is it to here?"

"From Harbortown to New Orleans? A little over an hour. An hour and fifteen minutes. How often will you need to bring him?"

"Every five weeks for two years. If nothing else goes wrong."

"Nothing else will go wrong. What did the doctor say?"

"That it's bone-marrow cancer. That the chemo's going nicely. So why did he have to go and break two vertebrae in his back?"

"Abe said himself that wasn't anything new. The doctors will take care of it. He'll be alright."

"'Til something else goes wrong. Something else breaks down..."

She told me in a frightened voice that Abe was tired all the time. She asked if my mama, who died of cancer, had been tired all the time. The room filled with darkness. I didn't make a move to turn on the lamp. I watched shadows of a dogwood tree move across the wall like giant spiders crawling slowly. Outside, a car trunk slammed.

"Mama was very weak," I said. "But that was from the drugs. That's why Abe is tired. From all the powerful drugs."

She began crying. "I hate for my children to see their daddy like this..."

Three months later, I parked by the side of the funeral home adjoining St. John's Catholic Church in Harbortown. My cousin, Elie, stood outside the church. I assumed he'd been appointed to stand there to greet the mourners. He hugged me; we talked. Inside, I made my way toward Meredith. She was seated in the front row, no farther than six feet from the open casket. I hugged her, told her how sorry I was. Serenely, she looked at me; she said how glad she was to see me.

Since Hurricane Camille had blown away the original structure in 1969, St. John's had been rebuilt to resemble a red brick bomb shelter. An abundant display of roses adorned the altar and smaller arrangements were dispersed throughout. Sally Ann and Blue sat in the front pew next to Meredith, with Meredith's children on the other side of her. The priest, a man in his sixties, commenced to give the eulogy:

"Abe wasn't the type who appeared on the front page of the newspaper to publicize his good works." He spoke with an Irish accent. "He didn't advertise his good work. But God knew." Pause. "And the people he helped in his practice knew. Abe was a good man. And I believe his life was prolonged by having his family by his side. His eyes would light up whenever he'd see Meredith and Melanie and Edmund..."

We departed the church as someone sang *Walk Around Heaven All Day* and drove in a procession toward the cemetery. It was supposed to be closed because of Armistice Day, and Frankie had to call the town mayor to ask him to keep it open for Abe's internment. The sky was a vibrant blue, the air in the chilly 50s. All my relatives gathered before the grave: my brothers; the A-Baki family; May; her sisters and brothers; Sally Ann and her family; Rima and Ed from Dallas. As I walked away, the others chanted prayers, and there was a moment when I glanced back at them to freeze this memory in my mind.

All around, breathless light, an all-embracing loneliness creeping over them on that day so very long ago.

~

I looked down at the darkened street below the celestial sky. A hushed loneliness enveloped Oretha Castle. It felt like a cemetery where prayers had been said before, one by one, everyone walked away—except for me and Blue. Maybe we weren't meant to know what we never knew. Maybe we were meant to be grateful for what we had and move on and never look back.

I stepped back into the bedroom, shut the gallery window, and tiptoed downstairs. I got myself a beer, hunted through the CDs, and put on Michael Bublé's *Crazy Love*. Death was creeping through the shadows and edges of the room, pouring out onto the sidewalk, seeping into my memory, filling up my brain, warning of what was to come when I didn't even know it. I listened throughout the night. The music was beautiful. In the nascent morning, I left without telling her.

CHAPTER 22

J took a shower after work and tried on several dresses, settling on an old standby—an absinth-green silk one that broadened my shoulders and slimmed my hips and made my waist look like next to nothing. I stepped into my black pumps and locked the door to my house.

I'd had to stay way late at work. It couldn't be helped. The speakers for the symposium had been calling and e-mailing all day, checking on last-minute arrangements, and there were details to be worked out with the hotel and a million other things to do. And so I was late leaving my house, shutting the door a little after eight o'clock, to drive to the Café, bearing a gift for Blue.

I parked my car on Oretha Castle, in the next block past the Café, and paused to take in the Gatsby-like atmosphere. Someone had decorated the orange tree with colored lights. The gallery was also lighted. Someone had placed little tables and chairs on the sidewalk and porch, linen cloths covering them. Outside, inside, and everywhere were lanterns, balloons, lighted candles, and fresh flowers: pansies, snap-dragons, calendulas, and sasanquas. Torrential rains falling all day had tapered off around six o'clock. The temperature was in the high 60s. A dense fog blanketed the street.

It was like a ghost haunting Oretha Castle, giving off a surreal, supernatural glow.

Inside, the Café beamed with colors, bright lights strung across the ceiling, banners welcoming everyone in three languages: English, Arabic, and Spanish. And I could tell Alejandro had worked extra hard whipping everything into shape for the long-awaited celebration.

And now it had arrived.

Two massive cast-iron chandeliers looked impressive hanging from the ceiling. And Alejandro's paintings adorned every wall. One showed a phantom figure, white-robed and winged, a human skull nestled at its feet. I figured it must be Saint Michael, the archangel, field commander of the Army of God. And there were paintings of the Madonna and Che Guevera. A faux skeleton sat on the elevated back frame of the bar alongside a miniature antique car with a license plate, "Mexico."

Behind the bandstand, a colored mural. I can only describe it as Alejandro's interpretation of an Air Force emblem. The wood-paneled walls had been painted red. A bicycle hung from the rafters. The room looked unique—magnificent, original—as only Alejandro could create it. (I knew this couldn't be Blue's artistry.) And it thrilled me and delighted me.

The smell of food wafted through the air.

In the kitchen, Elenita and Lauriet busied themselves placing chilaquiles on silver platters and something I recognized as *fa'toy'yeh b'sbaanegh* on other platters. These were the same gleaming silver platters Blue had used long ago for her New Year's Eve parties.

And there she was.

Hands on hips, she was directing Gaynelle. She had her

back to me so that I couldn't see her face. She was wearing a pale lavender dress with a string of pearls around her neck. And as she turned to face me, she had the look of someone going somewhere special, only it wasn't a place she wanted to be.

Her face reminded me of a movie I'd seen once. In it, a young woman smears all kinds of creamy foods all over her face, and, from the look in her eyes, I could tell she was demented. Blue had her makeup appropriately arranged, if a bit too much. She was certainly dressed properly, if a little overdressed. Her rouge was streaked, and if you looked into her eyes, you could see tragedy written there. "Bereaved" might be a better word to describe my aunt that night, as if her heart had been ripped out of her. I lay down my gift, walked out of the living room, unable to bear facing her. Behind the fog peeked a golden moon.

Coming our way, Odessa carried a chocolate doberge cake, rectangular and three-layered, and, as she ascended the porch steps, I saw that it read, *Happy Birthday, Blue.* Someone followed behind her, carrying a yellow cake: *Happy Birthday, Café Dryades.* And there was Alejandro, parking his jeep. He got out, eyes downcast. He looked handsome with his sturdy build and proud demeanor and intense dignified expression. But you could sense his discomfort as he made his way toward the building, probably dreading playing host for the night, standing beside Blue, greeting everybody.

And there was Otavio, arriving with his wife. They got out of a cab, walked self-consciously down the sidewalk, shy and sweet and formal, a bit afraid, holding hands, devoted to one another. I'd never seen him in anything but dusty jeans. But this night he was wearing a black striped suit jacket, black striped suit pants, a white cotton shirt, and a purple silk tie. He'd gone to considerable expense to fly his wife down from Atlanta. And though Blue had begged to help him with expenses, he wouldn't let her pay. He was doing it to honor her on her special night. Evandro arrived with his family. His wife had driven all the way from Connecticut with their three sons.

And there was Irma Thomas, soul queen of New Orleans. She was getting out of her car. She and her husband had parked in the lot adjoining the Frederick Douglass Center. Odessa hurried back across the street to greet them and escort them to the Café. And Fredy Omar arrived. He was a native of Honduras and had a beautiful tenor voice. He played gigs all over town—Café Brasil, Snug Harbor, Rock 'n' Bowl, House of Blues—and was Alejandro's best bud. I never knew the circumstances of how the two happened to meet. They were both great artists in their own ways, and so I wasn't surprised they got together. Walking behind him were members of his band, from Colombia, Puerto Rico, Cuba, and Peru. They'd played with him for years. Alejandro met them outside, escorted them in. Through the open door, I saw them head for the bandstand to set up their musical instruments.

And everybody else arrived. They walked in grudgingly. They stood beside the walls like frightened boys at a sock hop, some of the Latinos Alejandro had invited looking sullen and resentful at having to mingle with gringo strangers. Then Odessa's guests arrived. They too stood against the walls, opposite the Latinos, or hovered together in booths, silent and estranged.

You could sense their irritation at having to attend a party for some old dressed-up White lady they didn't even know. But they were doing it for Odessa. Odessa got them here—had coerced them into coming. Odessa wouldn't hurt Blue, this party was too important—it was her birthday, after all—but you could swallow the tension, the restlessness and impatience, waiting for it to be over, the coerced, irritated, not-wanting-to-be-here strangeness and gloominess filling every particle of space. And I wondered what kind of Mother of God would play such a trick on Blue, to condone this nightmare of a horror opera after all her loyalty and self-sacrifice.

You could see it in Lennus.

He trudged behind his mother as they entered the Café, saved only by the trailing waft of her loving kindness from a total meltdown. Alice spotted Blue and hurried over to greet her, hugging her, and Blue clinging to her, laying bare all the sorrow contained within her broken heart.

And then Russell Kalify arrived. The spindly orchestra leader stood at the door, a thin, giraffe-like, amiable figure with a beak nose and moon eyes. He was smartly dressed. You had to admire his sense of style: grey suit jacket, grey pants, black cotton graphic T, black wool plaid scarf. He searched the faces of everyone in the room and realized they were mostly strangers, and then spotted Blue greeting other guests, and after they drifted off and she stood alone, bereft and devastated, the unmistakable aura of hopelessness about her, he glided over and took her hand. She looked like she wanted to cry, she was so happy to see his friendly face. Too soon, he wandered off. He grabbed some champagne and settled by the bar, watching as the others drifted in.

His eyes lit up. He'd spotted May at the door, anxiously looking around, flanked by Soraya and Johnny. He practically leaped off his stool and ravenously embraced her. He was set for the night. But Johnny wasn't. Johnny had read the crowd. He'd sized them up and braced himself against the tension that threatened to divide and spread and mutate into something far worse.

They remained standing against walls—Latinos, African-Americans, a few Lebanese—gawking, grumbling, restless and bored, without so much as a thought of getting to know each other.

They were dressed in all kinds of ways: tee-shirts and jeans, suits and ties. A few brought gifts and dumped them in a corner. Lennus had eluded Alice and snuck out, probably to smoke a joint. Blue was trying her best to be the attentive hostess, going one by one to every guest, saying over and over, "Thank you for coming," pretending, carrying on, despair saturating every pore, permeating the room like the riverine fog outside.

Alejandro had given up. He stood behind the bar mixing drinks, wiping glasses, solitary and aloof. Lauriet and Elenita scurried about with their silver trays, offering food and champagne. And then Fredy Omar spoke. He was dedicating the first song to Otavio and Evandro. They, after all, helped build this Café. And then he began to serenade them with a Brazilian song. The room grew quiet. Lured by the tender, haunting melody, Otavio got up from a back booth and took his wife's hand and, together, they walked shyly to the dance floor.

They danced alone, unaware of anyone else, in love as if on their honeymoon. I could feel the crowd stir. And then Evandro got on the dance floor with his wife, and moments later, Russell slid out of his booth and extended his hand. May, who'd been sitting beside him, blushing and hesitating, her first instinct to decline, was overcome by her party self, the exhibitionist that she was.

She stood up, took his hand, and walked with him to the dance floor. The song was *Tempo Interno*, a light, driving Afro-Brazilian beat, almost holy in its evocation of the fragility of time. *"I still have time to be alone... peace is the sound of silence..."* The two of them did the samba. Their virtuosity and delicacy took over the floor with a passion and raw longing that seemed to stun the crowd, and the two of them looked great together. He was eighty and she almost that age, but they were relaxed and sure and happy. The last strains died out, ephemeral, euphoric and sad, floating through the air, and finally gone, and then a second or two of silence before Fredy Omar burst forth with the Isley Brothers' *Twist and Shout*.

Some of the younger Brazilians started dancing among themselves. Russell got down, dancing like he'd done it practically since the age of one, elbows working, knees bent, pounding one foot and then the other, and May, looking into his eyes, catching the attitude, getting low, bending knees, shimmying her frail shoulders. And Odessa got on the floor, the queen of center stage, acting like she'd done it at least a million times, both hands raised, shaking them like tambourines, eyes closed, stomping one foot and then the other, thrusting hip, thrusting hip. *"Shake it shake it shake it, baby..."* And then Alejandro, having a change of heart, went looking for Blue and, finding her, walked over and took her hand. It was Blue's initial response to wildly refuse, but Alejandro wasn't having it, and finally winning out, he led her to the floor, and together they joined the others.

At that very moment, the A-Baki's walked in. They'd driven all the way from Mobile, Alabama, for Blue's celebration. Of all my cousins, they were the most fun, most loving, generous, hell-raisers all of them. Lured by the driving beat, they headed for the dance floor, breaking out into wide grins. And the most surprising of all: Lennus. Mellow, no doubt, from all that pot and booze, he floated over to Elenita, took her tray, and put it on the bar. By no means reluctant, they weren't about to waste time, rattling arms, stretching out feet, pounding, head shaking, hardcore... *"shake it shake it shake it, baby... work it on out..."* And that's when the music changed.

Irma Thomas took the stage. She broke into a '70s tune—

from the glory days of disco. "... *I love the nightlife, I got to boogey...*" Sassy—"*I want some ackshaunnnn...*" and everybody on the floor, led by Odessa, whose tambourine hands never stopped, and MaryLynn A-Baki, smack in the middle of everything, jerking arms, stomping feet, her brother, feet wide apart, stomping, stomping, head shaking like his hair was set afire, and then Fredy Omar calling out, "This one's for Alejandro."

The song was called *Cuba*. I'd never heard it in my life before. A perfect synchrony of maracas and drum, it took you to the shores of Cuba and wild dancing nights. Quick, short, precise, Alejandro and Blue, oddly, were the perfect pair—Alejandro smooth and expert, and Blue, who'd probably never done it in her life, under the spell of the salsa beat, using her feet to move, but not move, just digging in, causing hips to roll and head to sway, perfect and classy, beautiful and wonderful. And Odessa grabbing Lennus, who looked like a young pro, confident, poised, knowing how to move his hands and feet, and the pianist exploding like a crashing race car, taking us into the stratosphere, and Lauriet and Elenita twirling. *Cuba... quiero bailar la salsa...*" And once again it was Irma's turn.

"This one's for Blue—happy birthday! We love you!" And everybody shouting, "*We love you!*" The trumpet and drums swung into action as Irma began singing, "*Just like a blind man I wandered alone, worries and fears I claimed for my own, then like a blind man that just got back his sight, praise the Lord, I saw the light...*" It was May and Alejandro this time, Otavio and Blue, Russell and Alice, Elenita and Lauriet. Then the trombone began wailing, holding the long note, and the band shifting into *Down by the Riverside*. And that's when Odessa completely lost control. She was shaking her head, stomping her feet, strutting, strutting, beating the air and—for one solid moment—pandemonium broke out.

That's when they let go with *When the Saints Go Marching In*, with Russell second-lining out the door into the street, tripping, tripping light, carefully down the steps, shimmying his shoulders, and everybody following—straight into the foggy night, into the dark streets of Oretha Castle. I will keep this in my memory for the rest of my life: horns blasting, cymbals clashing, piano pounding as the erratic snaking line of moving body parts rambled down the Boulevard looking like they'd die if they couldn't dance—Russell, May, Lennus, Elenita, Alejandro, MaryLynn, Lawrence, and all the rest. The great lights of jubilation penetrating the scrim of fog with no reason for happiness but the night and the dance: Russell, shaking booty; Odessa, her wicked self, half down, sideways.

I was standing by the door, shaking it myself, when I felt a hand touch my shoulder. It was Blue. She was practically irradiated, eyes illuminated by sweet relief that seemed to vanquish all worry and make her feel young again. "I'm leaving," she told me.

I said, "Where are you going?"

She said, "To be with Sally Ann."

I said, "Not tonight. Wait 'til tomorrow."

She just kissed me and hugged me.

"You don't have to go tonight," I begged. "It's too hard to see tonight. Wait 'til *tomorrow*."

But she wouldn't listen, and I asked her to give a reason.

"She's my daughter," she told me, "and I have to be with her."

"But she has her own daughters," I shouted. "And she's got Meredith and Frankie. And Rima and Ed. You don't have to go tonight! *Wait 'til tomorrow*."

"But she *needs* me," she insisted. "She needs me *tonight*—"

And those were her final words.

In my drunkenness, I just assumed Alejandro was taking

her. But, still, I should have made sure, and I should have called Frankie, told him they were coming. I should have gone back into the Café and used the phone right then. I should have done a lot of things. But I didn't want to wake Frankie, didn't want to worry Frankie. I should have tackled her by the ankles and locked her in a closet. But this was the thing: I was having too much fun. I'll never forget the moment I looked out into the conga line, saw those lit-up faces and dancing feet, and on either side of them I did a double take because I saw the vacant buildings breathing— breathing out, breathing in—I swear to God I did, like some magical ultra-humans in Alejandro's paintings, waking up to the action like they'd only slept a single day instead of the last fifty years, the long nightmare over.

❧

I got a call at five. I don't know why it took them so long or how they even found me. I couldn't sleep; I was washing dishes, and I heard the phone ring. It was an eighteen-wheeler on the Interstate, past the Lake Pontchartrain twin span, somewhere past Slidell—an eighteen-wheeler going too fast and didn't see her in the fog, and she going too slow. She was driving by herself. This is something I'll have to live with for the rest of my life: I didn't do a thing to stop her.

❧

I, with my cousins, share ownership in the building. Things got so bad with Lennus that Alice made him live with Alejandro. Lennus does most of the chores, and Alejandro pays him a decent wage. They live in the Café. He sleeps in one of the rooms, and Alejandro in

Blue's large bedroom. Not surprisingly, they fight. Often, we hear shouting, with Alice and I just standing there, waiting for it to be over, for the great storm to pass, and that happens quite often.

Alejandro is like a father to him. He won't let him skip school, tries to take away his joints, won't let him cuss or swear. Lennus has needed this for a very long time, and we're beginning to see changes. There'll be other changes coming: Alejandro's son is coming to live with him. He's nervous about it—excited. I guess in a way his dreams have come true. He manages the Café he's wanted all his life and will soon have his son with him, two boys to take care of. It may not be in Mexico, but on Oretha Castle Haley Boulevard. But that's not so terrible.

The Café has regular customers now. The actors from the Frederick Douglass Center come to eat after their performances, and Russell comes over to get his fix of *kibbi nayye*, picking up May, bringing her along.

Sally Ann only lived six months. They operated on her the day Blue died, but they didn't take out the cancer. It had spread and so they sewed her up. And every once in a while, Frankie will drive over from Harbortown to eat *lahem b'ajeen*, which Blue taught Gaynelle to make. He comes over, I do believe, to pay his respects to her, sort of like someone at a grave, telling her he was wrong and sorry for the things he said.

The Faysal brothers, the ophthalmologists, come over occasionally, too. And that's quite a shocker. I never expected that. And on Saturday nights, when Fredy Omar does his regular gig, every Latino in Central City can be seen at the Dryades Street Café. Alejandro is teaching Odessa and Alice how to salsa, and they come over and bring their dates along, and Lennus just stands there, fuming, acting like their chaperone.

One evening when I didn't have anything much to do, a memory came back to me. I recalled the day, talking with Alejandro and me, Blue decided she'd name her building the Dryades Street Café. I thought it fitting at the time because dryads were female spirits who preside over groves and forests, as Blue would preside over her beloved Boulevard.

Wanting to know more, I looked up "dryad" in *The Encyclopedia Mythica*. According to Greek mythology, each dryad is born with a certain tree over which she watches. The lives of the dryads are connected with those of the trees; should the tree perish, then the dryad dies along with it. If this is caused by a mortal, the gods will punish him for that deed. The dryads themselves will also punish any thoughtless mortal who would somehow injure the trees. I looked up from what I was reading, and a chill ran through me. I thought how true my instincts had been, that it wasn't too far-fetched to believe that Blue watched over the Café and the Boulevard itself, and still is watching now.

And I think she may be satisfied.

Last Saturday night, I looked around the Café and saw twenty Black customers dancing on the floor to the pulsating beat of *Cuba,* forgetting how they looked or what their feet were doing or who was there beside them, caught up in the fiery Latin rhythm, blending in with the olive skins and cinnamon as they danced with their shoulders shaking, hips gyrating.

And it dawned on me then that if I had been Blue (or Blue had been me), it would have been done quite differently, first pondering the implications of the project and then patting myself on the back for not going forward. And all the years would have passed without anything getting done, as I congratulated myself, adored myself, for not creating a catastrophe. But she must have lived by a different set of rules, heard some other voices in her head (Aunt Zaina's? Sitty

Yamine's?) as if it came naturally to push beyond the fear, edge forward on the high wire, brazenly beneath the stars, following the mystical voice of God, or the Mother of God, above the distant salty earth, thrusting forward, inch by inch, moving into eternity.

On that night when I looked around to see the vacant buildings breathing, as if I'd gone forward in time, I knew my sweet aunt had transcended death—of a street, a building, a family, of life and faith and love, of her own death and mine.

I look up at the distant stars while a cool breeze blows past me. And I'm not at all sure, but wouldn't be surprised, if within a year or two another café opened up, and then a coffee shop or jazz club. And I think, come December 10th, a full year will have passed, and it may be just time to think about a first anniversary party.

SPECIAL THANKS

I wish to thank my longtime friend Linda Stone, the co-owner of Casa Borrega, the famous Mexican bar/restaurant that once reigned over Oretha Castle Haley Boulevard and gave everybody lucky enough to eat, drink and dance there the best memories of their lives. My gratitude to Linda for her generosity and kind heart in letting me glimpse what it is like to take an empty building and, along with her talented co-owner husband, Hugo Montero, renovate it from scratch and bring it to glorious, music-loving life under the dancing stars of New Orleans. My very special thanks to John Jarrett, who was like a guardian angel to believe in my book and give it a good home.

ABOUT THE AUTHOR

Born in Gulfport, Mississippi, Vicki Salloum has lived in New Orleans for many years with her husband, the late Wayne Joseph Holley. In addition to her longer works, her short fiction has appeared in the anthologies *When I Am An Old Woman I Shall Wear Purple* (Papier-Mache Press, 1987), *Pass/Fail: 32 Stories About Teaching* (Red Sky Books, 2001), *Voices From the Couch* (America House, 2001), and *Umpteen Ways of Looking at a Possum: Critical and Creative Responses to Everette Maddox* (Xavier Review Press, 2006). She holds an MFA in creative writing from Louisiana State University in Baton Rouge.

At Silent Clamor Press, we seek to illuminate the human experience with excitement, elegance, and unflinching honesty. If this work has resonated with you—offering a profound journey or a new way of seeing the world—consider sharing your reflections with others. Your voice enriches the ongoing conversation that keeps literature vital and transformative.